THE SUNSET KID

Deadly bounty hunter Johnny Sunset roams the West. After killing two of the outlaw Bower brothers, he heads to Silver City to collect his reward money, but Moss Carver and his gang have stolen every cent from the bank. In order to collect his blood money Sunset must follow them to Deadman's Draw. However, unknown to him, two more Bower boys are trailing him with vengeance burning in their hearts. The Sunset Kid faces his greatest challenge ever . . .

MICHAEL D. GEORGE

THE SUNSET KID

Complete and Unabridged

LINFORD
Leicester

First published in Great Britain in 2010 by
Robert Hale Limited
London

First Linford Edition
published 2011
by arrangement with
Robert Hale Limited
London

British Library CIP Data

George, Michael D.
 The Sunset Kid. - - (Linford western library)
 1. Bounty hunters- -Fiction.
 2. Western stories.
 3. Large type books.
 I. Title II. Series
 823.9′2–dc22

 ISBN 978–1–4448–0663–2

Published by
F. A. Thorpe (Publishing)
Anstey, Leicestershire

Set by Words & Graphics Ltd.
Anstey, Leicestershire
Printed and bound in Great Britain by
T. J. International Ltd., Padstow, Cornwall

*Dedicated with love to my
youngest daughter Candice Mary*

Prologue

Spirals of dust were lifted heavenward and into the blue cloudless sky off the hoofs of the powerful stallion as its master steered it towards the white-washed adobes. Over the aeons a shallow yet fast-flowing river had carved out a deep ravine through the otherwise arid terrain just below the town of San Carlos. The river itself marked the border between Texas and Mexico, but one man refused to recognize any man-made boundaries.

When he was on the trail of outlaws wanted dead or alive he followed wherever the trail led him. When the various reward monies totted up to an even $1,000 the notorious bounty hunter became blind to everything except executing the outlaws who had become his prey.

He had become known to most as Johnny Sunset yet others called him the

Sunset Kid. No one knew for sure what his true handle was but the word sunset meant those he chased were close to the end.

Once he caught up with those he pursued it was certain they would never see another sunrise.

Few knew who he actually was or where he had come from. All they knew was that he appeared like an avenging angel and dispatched those who had escaped the wrath of the real law. It was said that his almost angelic features belied the fact that he was totally merciless. Those who lived by the gun would surely die by the gun once Sunset had their Wanted poster and knew their value.

Sunset took no prisoners. Dead or alive meant dead. Like the mainly unmarked border which separated two countries, he refused to acknowledge the distinction. Dead outlaws were far easier to handle. They required no water or vittles and were better company. Apart from attracting buzzards, flies and vultures, that was.

So it was as Sunset drew rein in the dusty border town just after dawn. He stepped down from his tall, sturdy mount, dropped his reins and entered the aromatic cantina set less than fifty yards from the shallow river. The beaded curtain made an almost melodic sound behind him as he paused and allowed his eyes to adjust to the unfamiliar place and those within its confines.

Every eye was upon the tall slim figure when he walked across the sawdust-covered floor to the bar and rested his gloved right hand upon its damp surface.

To those who watched from beneath the brims of sombrero and Stetson alike he did not appear to be anything special. There seemed to be no threat in his low, whispering voice. He wore just one gun on his left hip. None of the patrons of the remote cantina could have imagined that they were looking at one of the most deadly gunmen in the West.

Sunset curled a finger and drew the

tanned man towards him without a single word being uttered. The barman looked up at the face. It was smooth-skinned and without scars.

'What you want, señor?' the man asked.

Sunset pushed his right hand in his shirt and pulled out a crumpled wanted poster. He shook it out and showed it to the barman.

'You seen these critters, amigo?' Sunset enquired in a hushed tone. 'I'm hunting these men!'

The man who dished out hard liquor and warm beer for a living could not read the English words on the poster but he could make out the crude photographic images and the price on the outlaws' heads. To men in this desert land $1,000 was a fortune.

'I see them!' He nodded as the bounty hunter returned the poster back into his shirt.

Sunset leaned closer. 'Where?'

The man looked coyly at the bounty hunter. 'You give me twenty dollar and I will tell you!'

Sunset nodded. He then grabbed the frayed shirt-collars and violently hauled the barman off the ground until his fat belly rested upon the wet counter. Their noses touched. Their eyes locked together.

'I'll ask you again! Where are they?'

The man gulped but knew there was still money to be made.

'Ten dollar?'

Sunset released his grip. The man fell backward. His sandals hit the ground and he steadied himself.

'Five dollar maybe?'

The bounty hunter shook his head and pulled three silver dollars from his vest pocket. He placed them down between them and stared hard at the shorter man.

'Three bucks!'

The barman nodded and scooped up the money as quickly as he could. Sweat dripped from his face as he raised a finger and pointed at the ceiling above their heads.

'They're up there?' Sunset asked. His

blue eyes searched the cantina until they lit upon the simple mud-brick steps.

'*Si!*' The barman replied. 'They rent room from me for last two days!'

Sunset slowly flicked the leather safety loop off his gleaming Colt .45's hammer. His left hand lifted the gun in its well-oiled holster, then allowed it to fall back again. He turned and looked at the other men seated inside the cantina. They were all staring at the tall figure with bemused curiosity.

'You a bounty hunter, *señor?*' the man behind the bar asked. 'You come to kill them?'

'Yep!' Sunset answered. His boots began to head straight for the steps he knew would lead him to the upper floor and the men he sought. His spurs rang out a deathly tune that many men had heard a few moments before they encountered Sunset and death.

'What is your name?' The barman asked.

The handsome face looked straight at

the barman. 'They call me Johnny Sunset!'

A united gasp went around the cantina.

'The Sunset Kid?' the barman stammered.

'Yep!'

Within seconds every man inside the quiet drinking-hole had gone, the rattle of the beaded curtain the only indication that they had ever been there.

Sunset walked up the steps slowly. Like a cat he listened and looked for any hint that those he chased would not turn the tables on him.

When he reached the upper floor a solitary door stood between him and the room he knew the outlaws occupied. He drew his gun and cocked its hammer with his thumb. There was sound inside the room. The sound of movement.

Sunset raised his right boot and kicked with all his power. The door shattered like matchwood, though its hinges somehow clung to the frame. But it was enough for him to see them.

The Bower brothers were reputed to

be as dangerous as any of their more famous contemporaries, yet Johnny Sunset had no fear of them. Even when both men dragged their guns from their holsters and began fanning their hammers he did not doubt his own ability to achieve his goal.

They were his.

Their bounty was his.

Even when the gunsmoke filled the small room and he could no longer see them, Sunset knew it would be he who tasted the fruits of victory. The lead had shattered what remained of the door and its frame but Sunset did not return fire.

Only when the shooting paused did Sunset throw his lean body through the acrid, blinding gunsmoke into the room. He rolled over and landed on his boots. The smoke swirled upward, then he heard the noise out in the street.

The bounty hunter rose, rushed to the open window and saw the men disappear into an alley opposite. They were heading for the river, he thought.

Sunset raised a boot on to the windowsill. He leapt out and landed on his saddle. He scooped up the reins with his right hand, dragged the powerful stallion around and then drove both spurs into its flesh.

Now it was a race.

A race between two men on foot with a sixty-feet advantage and a rider atop one of the most powerful horses in Texas.

A race to see who would reach and cross the river first. The black horse thundered around the buildings, leaving a cloud of choking dust in its wake. More bullets came at him. This time they were too close. Sunset had felt the heat of the lead. The Bower brothers' aim was getting better.

He hauled back on his reins, and saw the men throw themselves out of sight down into the ravine. Again Sunset held his .45 in check. He spurred once more and urged his horse on.

The sound of splashing water filled Sunset's ears as he reached the edge of the steep ravine. He allowed his mount to jump down into the shallow water. Plumes of water cascaded up over him and his wide-eyed mount. Sunset steadied himself on his saddle when another bullet whizzed past his head. He spurred once more and hung on as the mighty stallion charged through the river.

Then he saw them.

The Bower brothers had reached the other side.

They were in Mexico.

Sunset spurred even harder.

The tall black stallion ploughed on like a locomotive. The outlaws were standing on the dry embankment laughing at him as he drew closer and closer. They continued laughing as they shook their spent casings from their guns before reloading.

The horse cleared the river and rode up the embankment. Its master reined in and glared down at the pair of outlaws he saw as nothing more than the $1,000 they were worth.

'Ya in Mexico now, Sunset!' Lane Bower laughed.

'Ya can't touch us here!' Rufe Bower added.

The Sunset Kid gave a slow nod and then looked at them both from beneath the wide brim of his hat. He pushed his Colt back into its holster and smiled.

'I'm still gonna kill you both though, boys!' he whispered.

The smile evaporated from the outlaws' faces. They looked into the face of the bounty hunter and suddenly realized that he was not joking.

'Ya can't kill us here!'

'I can and I will!' Sunset replied.

As though they shared the same brain both brothers swiftly raised their reloaded guns again. Just as their fingers curled around the cold steel triggers they saw Sunset's left hand return to his holstered gun's grip.

The bounty hunter fired twice. Both bullets cut into the wanted men dead centre. They buckled and shot into the sand just before their faces hit the ground.

Johnny Sunset returned his smoking

weapon to its holster, then pulled his rope from the saddle horn. He made a loop and spun it a few times before sending a lasso down over the dead men. It encircled their twisted forms. He tightened the rope until he had them secured, then he turned his horse and spurred.

It was as if every eye in San Carlos were watching the bounty hunter as he towed the pair of lifeless outlaws back across the river towards the Texan town.

A man with a star pinned to his shirt watched the bounty hunter closely. When Sunset reined in beside him the sheriff looked down at the pair of bodies.

'I claim the bounty on these bastards, Sheriff!' Sunset whispered.

The sheriff shrugged and rubbed his chin. 'That's kinda awkward, Sunset! We ain't got a bank here no more! I'll have to give you a scrip to take to Silver City! They'll pay you your blood money there!'

Johnny Sunset threw the rope to the ground.

'Where is this Silver City, Sheriff?'

'Ten miles east of here!'

Sunset dismounted. 'I'll head on out after I water and grain my horse!'

'Good!' the lawman muttered.

1

The six outlaws had spent the previous hour oiling and loading their arsenal of weaponry in readiness. Then they waited high in the rocks which overlooked Silver City until the sun had started to set. Only then did Moss Carver and his followers mount their horses and steer them down towards the sprawling Texan settlement. Dust filtered up into the dry air off the hoofs of the half-dozen horses as they made their way down through the rocky terrain towards the sunbaked range.

Their long dust-caked trail coats hung from and covered not only most of their saddles but the gleaming array of guns and rifles with which this small army was laden. They still resembled the soldiers they had once been as they trailed Carver, the seasoned outlaw, as he steered the fastest route down towards the almost flat expanse of lifeless land.

Carver was a man who had learned his brutal trade the way most outlaws had during the war. Killing and purloining had become second nature to the forty-year-old man. They were things he was good at. They were skills he had honed like a straight razor during the five or so years following the end of the conflict.

The riders who followed Carver were men who had seen death close up. It held no fear for any of them. Each felt that his survival of the bloody conflict was testament to his own immortality.

Carver's training of them to be merciless had proved to be the most remunerative lessons they had ever learned. Their loyalty to and trust in the hardened outlaw who led them had now become second nature.

By the time the riders reached the flat land below the foothills it was almost dark. Carver had checked his half-hunter against the sun's dying embers long before they had reached the arid landscape.

Carver knew that they had thirty minutes to reach the bank before it closed. He had timed the ride between Silver City and the rocky outcrop earlier that morning.

They were on schedule.

The six horsemen spurred and drove on towards the place where streetlights beckoned like sparkling fireflies. Carver had learned long ago that a bank was at its most vulnerable in the minutes before closing.

It was also the time there was the most cash in its tellers' drawers.

For the entire duration of the war Carver had never managed to be promoted. Yet if ever there was a man who should have been made an officer, it was he. He was a true leader. Men followed where he led, listened to what he said and obeyed without question.

No battlefield general had ever been given such blind devotion from his men as had Moss Carver.

As the town grew ever closer Carver became more confident. Every one of his bank robberies had succeeded because it was planned with military precision. No detail was overlooked or ignored.

During the previous five years Carver and his gang had robbed nearly a dozen banks across three states and territories. They always managed to escape unscathed with their spoils. But fate was a fickle friend. Like a pendulum, it could swing in both directions. Some might call it luck and that was a coin with two faces.

One good, one bad.

Carver harboured none of these thoughts as he whipped the shoulders of his horse to urge greater pace. He had no doubts. No thoughts of failure, for this was like another battle. To survive you had to remain single-minded.

The riders drew closer to their destination.

Like so many other Texan towns, Silver City was a maze of streets which showed no true design. If there was a main street it was not obvious. So many alleys and side streets twisted and turned in every conceivable direction.

Carver knew the fastest route to their goal. He had ridden through the busy town only once, that very morning, but its layout had been branded into his memory.

The horsemen rode in single file. Store-front windows were slow to light up. The outlaws used the shadows to their advantage. Darkness offered them a shield from prying eyes and deadly bullets. The riders eased back their pace as they passed a man carrying a long pole with a lighted rag at its end. The man was lighting the wicks of the streetlights, as he did every day at sundown.

Carver smiled to himself.

The man was headed in the same direction as he and his followers, which meant that the street where the bank stood would be dark long enough for them to complete their business.

18

After turning a corner Carver reined in as he reached the hitching rail outside the bank. Unlike many they had robbed before, this bank was mere brick and board. He swung the head of the animal around to face his men as they too stopped their horses.

Each of the expert thieves knew their individual duties. They had become like a well-oiled machine: a machine which robbed banks swiftly.

Carver threw his right leg over the horse's head and slid down to the ground. With a few stores' front windows casting their strange orange light across the hardened sandy street Carver looked at the faces of his men, as he always did when they were about to strike.

Any hint of fear in the cold-blooded faces could mean disaster to them all. Yet, as always, there was none.

Hope English was the oldest of the bunch; he remained atop his powerful stallion. His keen senses were alert as he watched everything around them for signs of trouble. English chewed on a plug of tobacco, knowing that it was his job to clear the streets of anyone who might try to stop his companions. His right hand drew his Colt and cocked its hammer in readiness. He held the gun against his thigh beneath the long tail of his jacket. English knew that he would only squeeze its trigger when his partners re-emerged from the bank with their plunder.

Carver nodded at English.

English winked and spat a lump of black goo on to the ground at his side. Words were not needed for men who had always known that each depended for his survival upon the other.

The four younger horsemen dismounted as one. Carver nodded to each of them in turn as they went about their well-rehearsed rituals.

Ben Fargo walked across the street with Sol Muller at his shoulder, their horses in tow. The two men tied their reins to a hitching pole and stepped up on to a boardwalk, which offered them a perfect view of the bank opposite. They kept their rifles hidden under their long trail-coats. They watched. The weapons would not be brought into action unless things went wrong. In the previous dozen robberies that had never happened.

With saddle-bags over their shoulders, Vin Egan and Shale Davis pulled their Winchesters from their scabbards and moved to either side of Carver as the determined outlaw pulled his own gun from its holster.

'C'mon!' Carver said in a low drawl.

The three outlaws walked to the bank's boardwalk, pulled their bandannas half up over their faces, then stepped up on to its weathered surface. Carver reached down, turned the well-worn doorhandle and entered with his men.

The bank was within minutes of closing.

The three tellers and the bank's manager looked as though they had had a very busy day and were ready to lock up. Carver glanced at the wall clock.

It was three minutes before six.

He indicated to Davis and Egan before moving across the room and vaulting over the low wooden rails to where the rotund manager sat beside his desk.

'This is a hold-up!' Carver snarled.

'What the . . . ?' The manager gasped as the barrel of the Colt was thrust under his jaw and pressed into the double chins. The cold steel made him fall silent as his eyes darted to the two other men with their rifles in their hands.

Davis slid the bolts both top and bottom to lock the door, while Egan pulled down all of the green window- and door-blinds.

'Hands high!' Carver yelled out.

Each of the tellers sent his arms straight up towards the stained ceiling.

Carver stepped back. His eyes glared at the seated figure who was shaking with fear.

'Get every damn cent in this bank

bagged up, fatman!'

The manager rose to his feet and waved at the tellers. 'You heard him! Get the money out of the drawers and into bags!'

Egan threw their empty saddle-bags over the screen to the trio of terrified men.

'Fill them satchels!' he growled from behind his bandanna.

Carver glanced at the tall safe set against the back wall. It was a large creature, big enough for even the tallest of men to walk into without the need to stoop. Its door was wide open. He moved towards it and stared into its dark interior. What greeted his eyes cheered him.

'How much money you got in there?'

The manager suddenly felt sick. Nearly every honest dollar in Silver City was deposited in the safe. He turned and looked hard at the man with the cocked Colt in his hand.

'I . . . I ain't sure!' he lied.

Carver gave an angry sigh and then

smashed the barrel of his weapon across the face of the fat man. The manager spun on his heels, then crashed to the floor. Blood spread quickly from his gashed head.

'Git over here, Vin!' Carver instructed Egan. The outlaw ran with his rifle still trained on the tellers as they filled the bags with cash from the counter drawers. He reached Carver, then paused.

'What, Moss?'

'Take a look in there and see how much paper money there is!'

'What about gold, Moss?' Egan asked. He walked towards the safe. 'We sure could use a heap of gold!'

Carver shook his head. 'Just paper money, Vin! Gold will weigh our horses down!'

Egan shrugged, grabbed a pile of money-sacks and entered the large safe. There was plenty of paper money stacked in neat piles along the shelves. He began to drag them quickly into his sacks.

It took less than five minutes to fill

every sack in the bank with the cash they desired. Carver was satisfied and waved for his men to unlock the street door.

'Give Hope the signal, Shale!' Carver ordered Davis.

As Davis stepped out into the darkness one of the tellers suddenly dropped below the long wooden counter. Neither Carver nor Egan noticed the first sign of defiance any of the bank workers had shown.

Then the teller got back to his feet with an Army Colt in his shaking hands. He aimed at the outlaws and squeezed its trigger.

The powerful gun blasted its deafening venom across the room. The kick sent the teller staggering backwards. The bullet cut through Vin Egan's back. He arched, then fell out of the building on to the boardwalk. The shot had caught him dead centre.

Carver and Davis spun around and stared at the three tellers in turn. It made no difference to them that only one had a smoking weapon in his hands.

'Kill them all!' Carver ordered.

'With pleasure!' Davis raised his Winchester and dispatched three deadly shots in quick succession. The tellers were knocked off their feet and sent hurtling into the back wall. Blood was splattered up the wall as the rifle bullets tore through them in turn.

Carver knelt and turned Egan's head towards him. He pulled the bandanna down and looked into the lifeless eyes. He rose back up just as Hope English started to fire his gun to clear the streets of anyone who might remotely be brave.

Davis jumped over his dead companion and ran after Carver to English and their tethered mounts.

'What happened?' English yelled to the two men who were frantically amounting their horse beside him.

'Vin's dead, Hope! Clear the streets!' Carver said. He looped the money sacks over his saddle horn and rammed his spurs into the flesh of his horse.

English began to fire his gun.

The sound of gunplay had echoed all around Silver City's narrow streets. Some men appeared from a saloon a hundred yards behind them. They began to fire their guns. With hot lead cutting through the dry air all around them, Fargo and Muller started to unleash their rifles' fury as they too mounted.

Both outlaws kept firing until Carver, English and Davis had galloped past them. Only then did they turn their own mounts and spur.

Within a few seconds the five outlaws were out on the range and whipping their horses to find a pace that no posse could match.

Hanging on to his reins as his mount thundered across the range, Carver dragged his bandanna down and spat. For the first time his perfect planning had gone sour and he had lost a man.

All because a scrawny bank teller

more used to handling pencils had found courage and a gun.

It was a grim lesson he would never forget.

2

The cold light of day made the spectacle no less sickening to the people who were drawn to the bloody scene like vultures to a fresh carcass. The bank was stained with the dried gore of the four victims who had fallen prey to Moss Carver's fury. The smell of death and putrid decay lingered within the four walls of the town's only bank as the undertaker and his assistant carried the last of the bodies out to the flatbed buckboard. People muttered whilst some cried for their lost loved ones. The bodies had already stiffened long before the morning sun had risen over the Texas town.

Things rotted fast in the harsh unforgiving land.

There had never been any trouble in Silver City before. Not even when the land had been rife with rich pickings.

The slaughter had come as a total shock to every honest soul who dwelled in the settlement, but it was the knowledge that most of their savings had been stolen that enraged the people more.

Sheriff Lou Favor was a man who had lived far longer than most of those who followed his occupation. There was a damn good reason for that. Favor did not like looking for trouble, and gathering a posse together and chasing the gang who had killed the four bank workers was looking for trouble. He had listened to the angry outpourings of most of the townsfolk for hours and, as the sun began to spread its light across Silver City, it dawned on him at last that their anger was starting to shift from the murderous bank robbers.

Now Favor was the villain.

Fists pounded on the office door as raised voices threatened and yelled abuse. But Favor remained inside his office, knowing that he was incapable of doing what they demanded of him. He was a man who could handle drunks on a Saturday night but anything involving gunplay was beyond his limited abilities.

The mayor of the large settlement barged his way into the weathered office and closed the door behind him. What Jonas Clute had to say was for Favor's ears alone.

The sheriff looked up from where he sat in his chair at the fiery expression carved into the mayor's face.

'Not you as well, Jonas?'

The mayor started to wave a finger at the lawman. A man he had ensured won the election.

'What on earth are you doing here, Lou?' Clute screamed out. 'I'd have thought that you would have managed to get a posse together by now and be a dozen miles away on the trail of them killers! What you doing sitting in here?'

Favor exhaled loudly. 'Did you see them dead 'uns at the bank, Jonas? Them tellers were all killed clean! One shot each in the chest!'

'So?'

Favor could not hide the sound of fear in his voice.

'That's mighty fine shooting for mere bank robbers, Jonas! Whoever done that weren't just robbers. They were skilled marksmen!'

The mayor moved round the desk and rested his rump on its edge. He looked hard at the sheriff.

'Are you telling me that you're scared?'

'Damn right!' Favor stood and rubbed his sweat-soaked neck with the palm of his hand, which he then wiped down his pants' leg. He looked out at the angry faces who were still raging and waving their fists at him. He turned and looked back at the mayor. 'I sure ain't happy about the thought of going after folks with carbines who can shoot that good! If I got a posse together we wouldn't get within a half-mile of them bastards before they picked us all off! Nope! Call me yella if you like but I can't see no sense in it!'

Clute walked to the burly man and grabbed his arm tight. 'I got you this job, Lou! I thought you had grit! Now you stand there and act like an old lady!'

Favor shook his head. 'I seen a lot of bank robbers in my time but not like these critters! They were like soldiers! Maybe that's what they once were, Jonas! You wanna go up against a bunch of soldiers who won't accept the war's over?'

The mayor released his grip.

'The town's lost nearly every dollar it has, Lou!' Clute explained. 'They only left the gold and that ain't enough to cover a quarter of the savings of the townspeople! You have to get it back!'

Favor rubbed his neck again. 'This is a job for a bounty hunter, not a regular lawman, Jonas!'

'What?'

The sheriff grabbed his hat off its stand and placed it upon his head of wet hair. He opened the office door and pushed his way through the jeering crowd until he could see the telegraph office. He strode towards it with the mayor hot on his heels.

'Where you going, Lou?'

'I'm gonna send me a wire, Jonas!'

'Who to?'

Favor glanced over his shoulder as he continued towards the telegraph office.

'The meanest bounty hunter I ever had me the misfortune to meet, Mr Mayor! I heard tell he's bin seen over in El Paso and if he is I could get him here in less than a week!'

'A week?' the mayor repeated. 'Them outlaws could be in Canada before that bounty hunter even gets here, you fool!'

Favor stepped up on to the boardwalk outside the telegraph office. He paused, turned and looked hard at the man who had trailed his every step. His attention then rose over the head of the mayor to the angry crowd of people who were now following them both.

'Can't you calm them idiots down, Jonas? They'll be stringing us up before the day's through at this rate!'

Clute turned and looked at them. Men and women with fire in their eyes. He felt his own heart start to pound the closer they got. He swung back until he was facing the brooding sheriff once more.

'We'll all be ruined, Lou!' the mayor snapped. 'If we don't get our money back we're as good as dead!'

Reluctantly the sheriff nodded in agreement. He clenched a fist and hit the wooden upright beside him angrily. Against his own better judgement he realized that his friend was right. There was no time to wait for a bounty hunter to arrive all the way from El Paso. He also knew that he had to show willing and form a posse to trail the men who had violated Silver City.

'OK, Jonas!' Favor shrugged. 'I'll do as you want! Just calm them folks down! I'll get us a posse together just like you said!'

The mayor beamed and faced the crowd. He waved his hands aloft and started to tell them the sheriff wanted

35

to get a posse together. He also lied and said that Favor had been waiting until the sun was high enough so that they had a chance of tracking the gang of killers across the rugged terrain.

Then Lou Favor saw the rider through the heat haze. He raised a hand and shielded his eyes against the powerful rays of the sun. He nodded to himself. Within seconds every other soul with eyes had spotted the horseman as he steered his mount towards them.

'Who is that, Lou?' Clute asked.

The sheriff shook his head and smiled. 'If that don't beat all, Jonas!'

'You know him?'

'That's Johnny Sunset!'

'Who in tarnation is Johnny Sunset?'

'Some call him the Sunset Kid!' Favor added. 'He's that bounty hunter I was gonna wire!'

'You mean the evil bastard you were talking about back at the office?' Clute gasped, raising his own hand against the bright sunlight.

'Yep!'

'What's he doing here?'

Favor looked at his friend. 'Maybe the Devil sent him!'

3

The black stallion walked powerfully along the centre of the street with its rider staring fixedly ahead at the commotion. Sunset was curious. His narrowed eyes were focused upon the crowd who were gathered around the man with the gleaming star on his chest. A man he had tangled with before. As the bounty hunter drew closer he could tell that something had happened in this remote desert town, something which had spooked every one of its inhabitants. His eyes darted to the bank and the wagon with bodies piled up on its flatbed.

There was no mistaking what must have occurred.

Sunset held his reins with the fingers of his gloved right hand as his left rested upon the grip of his holstered gun. The crowd parted as the black horse continued to walk towards the sheriff.

'Howdy, Kid!' Favor said sheepishly.

Johnny Sunset eased back on his reins. The stallion stopped and snorted. The horseman looked all around him at the crowd, which seemed to be made up of every section of the town's population. He pushed the brim of his hat back off his brow. Sweat-soaked blond hair fell to his eyes. Sunset stared at the men, women and children who encircled him. He then tilted his head and looked at the sheriff.

'Long time, Lou!' he muttered in a low drawl.

'I heard you were in El Paso!' Favor said as he stepped down from the boardwalk and looked at the magnificent mount.

'I had me some business over in San Carlos!'

Favor nodded. 'How come you came here? There can't be many rich pickings around this part of Texas!'

'I ain't here to visit!' Sunset dismounted in a slow fluid action. He led the stallion to the closest trough and dropped the reins to the ground. 'I killed two *hombres* over in San Carlos and they sent me here to collect my reward money!'

Favor glanced across at the anxious mayor. His eyes then returned to the bounty hunter.

'Ain't you gonna tie this horse's reins to the hitching rail, Kid?' The sheriff asked coyly. 'He might run off! I'd hate to see you lose such a valuable chunk of horseflesh!'

'He don't run off!' Sunset said drily. 'What happened over yonder?'

Favor cleared his throat and rubbed his neck. 'We had us some trouble last night at sundown!'

Sunset walked away from the crowd towards the wagon and the two men clad in long black funeral-parlour attire who were busily trying to place the body of Vin Egan on top of the bank-workers' corpses. The lawman and the mayor hurried behind the tall, lean figure as he strode up to wagon.

'I know that critter's face, Lou!' Sunset said, pointing at the outlaw as

40

he was thrown on top of the others. 'He's wanted!'

The sheriff stopped and stood beside the bounty hunter. He looked hard at the body with the huge hole in its chest.

'Who is he?'

'Name of Egan!' Sunset replied. 'He rode with a gang led by a varmint called Moss Carver!'

Favor shrugged as Clute reached them. 'I never heard of either of them!'

Johnny Sunset glanced at the man with the star. 'It figures! You really ought to look at them Wanted posters in your office once in a while!'

'Mr Sunset!' Clute chimed in. 'I'm the mayor and I feel that we might have a job for you!'

Sunset smiled briefly. 'I only came here to get paid for the vermin I killed over in San Carlos!'

'That might be a problem, Kid!' Favor said.

Sunset looked hard at the sheriff. 'Problem?'

'Lou's trying to tell you that the bank

lost all of its cash last night, Kid!' Clute explained. 'We can't pay the bounty money you have coming!'

Sunset turned his attention to the mayor. 'You telling me that Carver and his boys cleaned the bank out?'

'We only got some gold coin left in there!' Favor sighed.

'I don't like gold!' Sunset whispered. 'Too heavy! That horse cost me a lot of money and I don't figure on busting his back with gold!'

'There ain't a dollar bill left in there!' The sheriff pointed at the bank. 'We can't honour the reward money you're owed!'

Before Sunset could speak the mayor edged closer. 'My idea is that you go after this Carver varmint and get the bank's money back, Mr Sunset! We will gladly pay you all the bounty money once we have our money back!'

Sunset walked round the wagon and stepped up on to the bloodstained boardwalk. He stared into the bank and inhaled the stench of death which lingered. He turned and looked back at the two men, who could not take their own eyes off him.

'This don't sound like a good deal to me! I go and risk my life just to get the money I'm owed? Seems to me that I'm doing your job for you!'

'We'll pay you an extra five hundred dollars on top of the bounties of all the outlaws you bring back!' Clute said.

Sunset gave a long low sigh. He then looked straight at the mayor. 'Make it an even one thousand and you got yourself a deal!'

Clute nodded. 'Agreed!'

The bounty hunter raised a finger. 'On one condition!'

Both men stared at the lean, keen-eyed man. 'What kinda condition we talking about, Kid?' Favor ventured.

Sunset did not reply immediately. He looked over the heads of the two sweating men, then whistled to his horse. The black stallion raised its head from the trough, turned and trotted across the street towards him. The magnificent animal stopped beside the boardwalk and waited as its master threw his leg over the saddle and poked both boots into the stirrups.

'This is gonna cost you six thousand dollars, friends!' Sunset said.

'It is?' Clute gasped.

'Yep!' Sunset nodded. 'I figure that Carver and his boys are worth close to four thousand dollars alone! Add on the one thousand you're paying me and the thousand I'm already owed and that comes to six thousand dollars!'

'Is that the condition?' Favor asked.

'Nope!' Sunset gave a long look at the roughed-up street and the tracks of the outlaws' horses, which were still visible to a man who made his living tracking and killing. 'I want you to ride with me, Lou!'

'But I ain't no good with a gun, Kid!' the sheriff pleaded.

'I was just joshing, boys!' Sunset smiled. 'I ride alone!'

Before either man could say another word the bounty hunter gathered his reins up in his gloved right hand, swung the stallion around and tapped his spurs.

The muscular horse responded straight away. A cloud of dust kicked up off the hoofs of the black horse. It hung in the air as the citizens of Silver City watched the Sunset Kid thunder away.

'Reckon he can do it, Lou?' Clute asked.

The sheriff exhaled loudly and squinted at the mayor. 'You bet he can, Jonas! I'd sure hate to be them outlaws! Once the Sunset Kid gets your scent in his nostrils nothing can shake him off!'

Jonas Clute watched the lawman walk back toward his office as the crowd rushed towards him filled with countless questions about the lone rider. The mayor wiped the dust from his face and greeted them with a store-bought smile.

4

Leaving a cloud of dust in its wake the powerful thoroughbred stallion thundered through the tumbledown streets as its master stood in his stirrups. The bounty hunter was reputed to be the best tracker of men ever to have taken a breath and the sight of the still visible hoof-tracks left by the Carver gang proved a lure no hunter could resist. The rider whipped the shoulders of his mount until he swung around a corner and spotted something ahead which drew his curiosity.

Johnny Sunset eased his mount's pace by leaning back until he mimicked a taut bow waiting to release its deadly arrow. The ornate lump of metalwork which hung high above the tall weathered stable doors went entirely unnoticed by the locals but, to the infamous Sunset, it meant that a craftsman probably occupied the big building.

Sunset had nearly reached the last of Silver City's array of buildings when the skilfully wrought piece of metal stopped him in his tracks. Most livery stables were situated on the very edge of sprawling settlements, far away from the delicate noses of the town's even more delicate people. Those who lived near this large building did so because they had no other choice. The ramshackle wooden shacks looked barely fit to house hogs, let alone people. The stench from them was almost as bad as the massive pile of dung in the corral adjoining the livery.

The bounty hunter did not appear to notice the stench of poverty as his mount eventually stopped in the narrow lane between the cluster of buildings. His flared nostrils had already inhaled the aroma of death and decay this day.

Sunset stared upward in awe.

A large well-built man with gleaming sweat and grime-stained skin walked out of the stable and paused for a brief moment whilst his eyes adjusted to the daylight that greeted him.

Olaf Krugar stood and focused on the rider before him with eyes that had seen more than his fair share of people in his lifetime. This man was unlike anyone Krugar had seen before. The blacksmith rubbed the palms of his massive hands down his leather apron as he watched the rider dismount.

'You look at my little statue, mister?' Krugar asked in a voice which reflected his European origins.

'I sure am, friend!' Sunset whispered. 'You made that?'

'I make!' Krugar nodded.

'You sure can handle metal!'

'No one ever see it before!'

'Reckon Silver City must have a whole heap of folks who are kinda blind!'

Krugar was flattered. 'Thank you! My name Olaf!'

Sunset allowed his reins to fall to the ground and walked up to the man who was at least a few inches taller than himself.

'You got any skill in adapting guns?' the Sunset Kid asked as he made the long journey around the huge black-smith.

'I can change guns! Easy!' Krugar nodded and stared down at the pristine Colt in its holster on the bounty hunter's left hip. 'Big and small guns is all the same to Olaf! I learn in the old country how! But your gun looks mighty fine to me!'

Sunset smiled and turned back to his horse. 'Not my six-shooter, Olaf! I got me something else I want changed. By the look of that up there you're the man who can do it!'

Krugar plodded behind the lean figure. He watched over the bounty hunter's shoulder as Sunset opened the nearest satchel of his saddle-bags.

'What you got in there?' he enquired.

'Maybe this'll answer your question!' Sunset pulled out something wrapped in oilskin and turned back towards the muscular figure. He handed the parcel to the man and watched as Krugar's eyes lit up when he unwrapped it.

Krugar stared down at the object in his large hands. He studied it for a few moments, then looked back into the face of the bounty hunter.

'This is bit of shotgun! Fine work but not finished!'

Sunset nodded. 'I want you to finish it!'

'Where barrels?'

'Ain't got none!' Sunset stepped closer. 'I need you to make and fix two barrels on to that for me! One above the other to make the gun narrow! Can you do it?'

'Sure I can!' Krugar seemed to be weighing the object with his hands alone. His head tilted. 'This mighty light for even a shotgun with no barrels, stranger! Olaf never felt one so light before! I do not understand!'

'I took it from a man up north a couple of months back!' Sunset informed. 'He was making it but never got to finish it!'

'Why not?'

'I killed him!'

'That is good reason not to finish!' Krugar turned and walked back into the shadows of his livery stables. The heat from the forge filled its vast expanse. 'Tell me why you kill this man who was making this gun?'

Sunset wandered to the far side of the forge. He watched as Krugar placed the gun down next to the red-hot coals and started to pump the bellows. Sparks drifted upward.

'It's what I do! He was wanted dead or alive!'

Krugar shrugged and then looked straight at the figure before him. There was no sign of any judgement in his bearded face.

'You bounty man?'

Sunset nodded. 'Yep! They call me Sunset!'

'I have trouble finding enough metal to make barrels for this gun, Sunset! May take two or three days!'

The bounty hunter moved closer to

51

the man with the abundance of rippling muscles. 'I don't want long barrels for this thing, Olaf! I want them short enough to be holstered and worn like a six-gun!'

Krugar stopped pumping his forge. Both his large hands fell on to the side of the brick furnace of hot coals. He leaned forward as if immune to the heat.

'You want to wear this like a gun?'

'Yep!'

'You will need special holster made!' Krugar thought aloud. 'I can make such a holster for you! I make saddles and this is more easy than saddles!'

Johnny Sunset walked around the forge and nodded. 'So you can do it!'

'Ya!' Krugar smiled. 'Olaf get bored just making shoes for stinking horses all time! I will make this for you!'

'How long will it take?'

'Four hour!' Krugar said confidently. 'Maybe five!'

Sunset smiled. 'How much will this cost me?'

'Forty dollar?'

'Do it good and I'll give you fifty!'

Olaf Krugar beamed. 'You mighty fine little man, Sunset!'

Sunset walked back toward the sunlight. 'You don't know me too well, Olaf!'

5

Flies were everywhere. They knew a feast when they saw one and the area surrounding the livery stables was a banquet. The heat rose ever higher along the narrow streets which made up Silver City's less prosperous section. There were no shadows as the sun hung directly overhead. Just merciless heat. But the bounty hunter either did not notice or he refused to acknowledge it. If Olaf Krugar could stand an even greater temperature inside the building then Sunset would not complain.

The sound of the blacksmith's trusty hammer echoed out into the street. It continued to pound the anvil as Krugar worked relentlessly at his forge, creating the unique weapon Johnny Sunset desired. For more than three hours the bounty hunter had sat out in the blazing sun, preferring its blistering rays to the sickening heat which filled the livery stable.

Curious eyes had watched the stranger during those hours and soon word found its way back to the sheriff in his office at the other end of town. The lawman had thought that the deadly hunter of wanted men had long gone on his deathly pursuit of the Carver gang. Now he found himself wandering along the darker side of town towards the big livery stable and the figure who sat on the dusty ground with his back against the wall.

Men in Favor's profession knew that simply by wearing a tin star they risked their lives whenever they ventured away from the safety of their office. He had seen the looks and heard the bitter remarks long before he had spotted the seated man he sought. Favor was nervous and it showed.

The closer Lou Favor got to the man with the brim of his hat pulled down over his face, the more his heart pounded inside his shirt. Favor looked to the black stallion as though checking that this actually was the bounty hunter. The magnificent animal remained untethered close to its master.

A thousand thoughts raced through Favor's mind.

Why was Sunset still here?

Could even the greatest bounty hunter of them all possibly catch up with the ruthless killers now?

He ran his sleeve across his sweating brow and gave out a long, silent sigh. Sunset looked so ordinary yet the sheriff knew that his lethal skill was far from ordinary. Favor had seen him up close when he drew that Colt. He had witnessed the deadly accuracy of the man.

Johnny Sunset was many things but never ordinary.

The leg of the bounty hunter moved and stopped Favor's advance. He could still hear the taunting voices billowing out from the shacks which surrounded him.

'That you, Lou?' the muffled voice

asked from under the Stetson that covered the sitting man's features.

Favor was surprised. 'How in tarnation did you know it was me, Kid?'

With the sleek grace of a mountain lion, Sunset rose up from the ground and allowed the hat to drop into the grip of his gloved right hand. He shook it, then returned it to the crown of his head.

'I heard you limping along! There's no mistaking that limp of yours!'

'I limp?' Favor looked at his legs and then back at the man who was now approaching him.

'Yep!' Sunset nodded and placed a boot on the bottom fence pole before resting his arms on the top one. His eyes did not look at the lawman but considered the mounts in the corral.

Favor strode closer. 'What you still doing in Silver City? I thought you were hot on the tails of them stinking killers!'

Sunset's blue eyes darted to the man beside him. 'Don't go fretting none! I'll still catch them! I told you that!'

'But you left me and Jonas back at the bank three hours back!' Favor protested. 'Them outlaws have managed to ride for three more hours and you're still here! How come?'

Sunset did not answer. He swung around on his heels, drew the Colt and cocked its hammer in one swift action. He then blasted one shot across the street. As the gunsmoke cleared and the open-mouthed lawman blinked hard a man staggered out from between two of the shacks. He had a Winchester in his hands. He fell on to his face. A cloud of dust rose up from around the body.

'You got enemies, Lou!' Sunset said. He removed the spent cartridge from his smoking weapon and replaced it with a bullet from his belt. Favor watched as Sunset twirled the Colt back into its holster and returned his elbows to the fence pole.

'I . . . I never heard a thing, Kid!' Favor gulped. 'How'd you hear him?'

Sunset's eyes looked at the sheriff. 'I ain't deaf!'

Lou Favor edged closer. 'Wait on a minute, Kid! How do we know he was gunning for me? He might have bin gunning for you!'

'He's still dead!' Sunset whispered.

Favor rubbed his face again. 'You didn't answer me! How come you're still in town?'

'It's a good job I am or you'd be dead, old-timer!'

'OK! I owe you one! But answer me, Kid!' Favor snorted.

'Olaf's making me a gun!' Sunset reluctantly informed the lawman. 'Are you happy now?'

'You gotta gun!' Favor pointed at the Colt, then glanced across at the dead man. 'And it seems to work just fine!'

Sunset turned his head. 'A new gun, Lou! A special 'one of a kind' gun! Unique!'

The sheriff looked confused. 'You ain't feared that them critters will get away from you, Kid? They sure got themselves a real head start on you!'

'Nope! I ain't feared!' Sunset whispered. 'Them outlaws don't know it yet

59

but they're already dead! When I catch up with them they'll figure that out for themselves!'

Favor shook his head. He went to speak when a hand reached out and touched his vest. Sunset turned away from the lawman and looked long and hard at the open doors of the livery stable.

'Hear that?' Sunset asked.

'I don't hear nothing, Kid!' Favor shrugged.

'That's what I mean!' Sunset said in a low tone. 'Olaf's quit hammering!'

'What does that mean?'

Johnny Sunset glanced at his companion. 'I reckon he's finished making the gun!'

Favor moved fast to the bounty hunter. 'Now you'll head on out after them killers?'

Sunset returned to the wooden wall of the stable and lowered himself down gently until he was seated once more. He then pulled the brim of his hat back down over his face.

'Nope! I'm gonna get me a little more shuteye before I ride on out, Lou!'

'Why ain't you going now, Kid?'

'Olaf's gotta make the holster first, Lou! A gun ain't much use without a holster!'

Lou Favor turned and started the long walk back to his office. His eyes flashed at the pool of blood which had spread out from the man with the Winchester gripped in his dead hands. Favor's pace increased. Every few steps he glanced over his shoulder and stared back at the seated bounty hunter.

He was no wiser.

Men like Johnny Sunset could answer every question thrown at them and still leave their interrogator none the wiser.

But evidence that he had lost none of his prowess with his gun was lying back there. Favor walked faster. The voices had stopped mocking him but he knew there were a lot more weapons in this part of town.

The sheriff did not wish to become a

moving target for anyone else who might think they had call to kill him.

'I don't limp, Kid!' Favor yelled out at the top of his voice.

'Yes you do!' Sunset whispered to himself.

6

Some said that only the Devil would have created a place so hostile as Deadman's Draw. And only a fool would willingly ride into its whirlpools of sickening heat haze. Nothing this side of the bowels of Hell could kill quite so mercilessly as did the savage wasteland of burning rock and sand. It had become a place which even the most foolhardy of creatures avoided like the plague. Its sand was littered with the bleached bones of most who had come this way. Many were animal skeletons but not all. Some had once been men. Men who had come seeking gold and found only death. Others had been lost in their quest to find a safe route to the fertile West which men back East dreamed about and had branded the new Eden. Deadman's Draw remained uncharted, as did so many other places in the vast land of so many contrasts. Those who followed the maps made by men back East had no idea what lay within the confines of the lethal canyons and towering rock spires. A simple line on a piece of paper gave no clue of the danger posed by such places. It might never be truly known how many people the map-makers had sent to their deaths through ignorance of what lay out in the untamed regions of the well-named Wild West.

Yet for all its dangers a few men had managed to navigate its course and survive. Sometimes the threat of almost certain destruction can be better than the alternative. Especially when the alternative is the certainty of a rope with a noose at its end.

That was how Moss Carver had discovered the secret of Deadman's Draw. Fear of what lay behind was greater than the fear of what lay ahead. Few men had either the guts or ambition to drive their horses into the baking-hot canyons which were flanked by high sand-coloured rockfaces and towering boulders which defied gravity as they balanced high above the scorching sand below. But Moss Carver had done that several times now, with his followers close on his horse's tail.

He knew that anywhere that was feared as much as Deadman's Draw had to be the perfect place for outlaws to hide out in between jobs. No man-made fortress of either wood or stone offered better protection than this monolithic place.

Somehow Carver had managed to achieve the impossible.

He had led his men into the place where the very air itself seemed to burn the lining out of your lungs. A place where a man's eyes could bleed from the fine sand which blew constantly along its canyon.

All this and he had survived.

Three times previously Carver had used Deadman's Draw. This would be the fourth. They had not stopped spurring their exhausted mounts since they had left the carnage back at Silver City. When the features of Deadman's Draw could be seen in the late-afternoon rays of sunshine Carver stopped his horse and eased himself down on the fine sand.

The four other outlaws dropped to the ground and lay there, holding their reins in their hands.

Carver squinted hard from beneath the brim of his hat at the awesome vision towards which they were headed. Sweat flowed like rain from his brow as he contemplated the next few hours of their travails. Experience had taught him how to survive in this satanic landscape. It held no fears for him.

He knew how to outwit nature and all its traps. Traps which were each designed to kill those who dared to challenge their superiority.

Carver turned and looked at his saddle-weary followers. Even here the sun was unyielding and could destroy the unprepared. He removed his hat and beat the sweat from its bowl against his right leg.

'We ready to head on out again?' Carver asked them.

There was a mutual groan from the four men.

He looked to the south to what appeared to be little more than a small rise of blackened rocks rising slightly above the otherwise rolling dunes. It was roughly two miles from where they had paused and just to the right of the mouth of the canyon. Unlike his followers, Carver knew what the stained rocks really were. He had discovered their secrets by accident two years earlier when fleeing a posse that would not quit.

'C'mon, boys!' he urged.

Slowly they each got up from the sand and looked at the man who they knew had the knowledge to keep them alive.

'Take them dustcoats off your cantles and toss them over your saddles!' Carver ordered. 'It'll ease them butt sores!'

Carver held his hat high and used its brim to shield his eyes from the bright sunlight. His keen eyes searched the desolate desert behind them. Their hoof-tracks were the only things to cast shadows for miles.

'We being followed, Moss?' Shale Davis asked as he gave the last of his canteen's water to his mount in the bowl of his upturned hat.

Ben Fargo screwed up his own eyes and searched the flat expanse of sand as well. 'You'd have thought they'd have rustled up a posse after what we done back there, Moss!'

'I bet there ain't a real man in Silver City!' Muller snorted. 'Takes guts to tackle folks like us!'

'I don't see nothing to fret about, boys!' Carver said, lowering his arm. 'Ain't nobody on our trail but that don't mean there won't be!'

Sol Muller rubbed his haunches. 'I'm raw, Moss!'

'Me too!' Hope English nodded. 'This damn place ain't fit for man nor beast! How come we ain't headed north? They got trees up north and my

68

skin could sure use a hunk of shade right about now!'

Moss Carver waved a hand. 'Quit moaning like a bunch of old school-marms! Water these nags! We need them to get us to where we're going!'

English plucked his canteen off the saddle horn and unscrewed its stopper. He looked at Carver hard and long.

Carver turned and returned the look. 'What's eating you, Hope boy?'

'How much money do you figure we got here?'

'Enough!' Carver retorted. 'More than enough!'

English cleared his throat. The war had savaged and aged him far beyond his years. Every movement hurt for the man who was by far the oldest of the gang. 'Enough for me to quit this life, Moss?'

Carver patted English's shoulder. 'I know you ain't the man you was, Hope! Hell! None of us is, but that ain't no reason to quit!'

'I hurt all the time, Moss!' English

whispered. 'Ain't nothing on this old carcass that don't hurt! My legs are stiff and my shoulders ain't supple no more! I got to quit whilst I'm still able to walk, Moss!'

Carver looked into the eyes of the man he had waged war with long before they had turned to robbing banks for a living.

'You can't quit now, Hope! We need you! We lost Vin last night and I can't afford to lose another man! The gang won't survive without you!'

English stopped talking. He knew that there was no point.

The bedraggled men were drenched in their own sweat. It burned the flesh beneath their clothes but they knew that Carver would lead them to an oasis. An oasis that only he had ever managed to find.

One by one they mounted. Carver returned his hat to his head and stared at the bulging moneybags each of their horses carried. He gave a wry smile to himself before stepping into his stirrup and hauling his weary body back atop his horse.

'Follow me, boys!' he said cheerfully. 'You'll be drinking the coldest of beer and eating the best tinned vittles this side of El Paso within the hour!'

'If anyone else had said that I'd have figured he was plumb loco, Moss!' Fargo grunted as he and the others mounted.

'Let's get this troop moving!' Carver waved an arm.

The men wrapped their reins around their gloves and stabbed their spurs into the flesh of their animals. They trailed the man who led them with the knowledge that he would honour his promise.

The five horses started across the smooth sand.

Their shadows were long and getting longer the lower the sun sank in the blue, cloudless sky. Soon a million stars would be above them shining like diamonds on black velvet.

If the five riders had been able they'd have stolen even them.

7

The passing of time had not diluted the interest of the bounty hunter, who appeared to be sleeping but in reality was still aware of everything going on around him. Not even the slightest of noises was ignored by the man known throughout the southern states and territories as the Sunset Kid. Even with his hat over his face he was still able to see through the weathered bullet holes in his Stetson. For just over an hour since the nervous lawman had returned to the safety of his office the bounty hunter had drawn more attention than flies to an outhouse.

Now there was something else to ponder.

Heads in windows watched as the burly blacksmith walked proudly out from his stable with a smile so bright it could have illuminated even the darkest of streets. This was a man who had drawn on a lifetime of skill and now had the opportunity to show it off.

Krugar held the hand-crafted holster and its specially built weapon in his right hand and a steaming tin cup full of coffee in the other. The large man downed the beverage, then tossed the cup aside.

He kicked the nearer boot of the man lying on the ground.

'I finish gun and holster, Sunset!' Krugar announced loud enough to deafen most folks. 'Look see what Olaf done for you!'

Sunset pushed the brim of his hat back. He eased his lean frame up off the sand until he reached his full height. Before looking at Krugar, Sunset surveyed the shacks facing the livery stable. The body still lay where it had fallen and now was being feasted upon by the town's stray dogs. Sunset's eyes narrowed as he observed those who spied upon him. Heads suddenly disappeared when the watchers realized that they were also being watched.

He then turned his face toward the blacksmith. 'Let me see, big fella!'

Krugar nodded. 'You bet! A mighty fine job if I say so myself, Sunset!'

Even the low sun could not hide the workmanship from Sunset's knowing eyes. He reached out and took the holster in his hands. For a moment he did not speak. He simply admired the skill of the huge man before him. Then he slid the weapon out of its specially made holster and nodded even harder.

'This is better than I hoped!'

The blacksmith had made a shotgun which was no longer than his Colt .45. It weighed a little more than the handgun yet was still light enough to be drawn in a showdown. The barrels were one above the other. It gleamed.

Sunset's blue eyes darted up at the smiling face.

'You're a genius, Olaf! I never seen such work!'

Krugar looked bashful. 'I don't know what genius is but if it good then that is what Olaf is OK!'

Sunset returned the gun back to Krugar and swiftly unbuckled his belt. He handed it to the large figure. 'You hang the holster on my gunbelt, Olaf!'

The blacksmith did as he was told. He fixed the holster he had constructed to the belt and then gave it back to the bounty hunter.

Johnny Sunset swung the belt around his lean hips and did up its buckle. The newly made holster rested on his right whilst his Colt remained on his left. The younger man tested the shotgun a few times until satisfied he could draw it with his gloved right hand.

'Smooth action! This is gonna be damn useful when I catch up to them bank robbers!'

'You southpaw!' Krugar noted as he stared at the .45 on Sunset's left hip. 'I not see many gunmen who use left hand!'

Sunset nodded once more. 'I favour my left hand for speed but this gun you've made is for my slower right hand! I don't need speed with a gun like this!'

'Why you need such a gun? I hear that the Sunset Kid is fastest of all bounty hunters!'

'Like I said, sometimes it ain't speed you need, it's the abilty to blow a hole through a barn wall!' Sunset replied. 'Or cut a whole bunch of varmints in half with one squeeze of a trigger!'

The larger man shook his head. He had never killed a man in his life and could not understand the men who peopled his adopted land. He did not comment.

Sunset looked at his stallion. He had taken the saddle from the horse's back hours earlier and now the animal was well watered, grained and rested. 'I better get my horse ready for the long ride, I guess!'

Thoughtfully Krugar looked up at the sky. 'Be dark soon! You stay in town tonight?'

Sunset shook his head. 'Nope! I got me some vermin to catch up with! I like riding when it's dark! You can get the drop on even the most wily of folks when it's dark!'

'Bad men head down towards desert!' Krugar raised a hefty arm and pointed. 'Danger out there! No water for miles!'

'I'll need a packhorse! You got one that can carry half its own weight in waterbags, Olaf?' Sunset enquired. 'If'n I can't find water then I'll take it with me!'

'I got one mighty strong horse!' Krugar was about to turn when he felt the hand of the bounty hunter on his forearm. He stopped and looked at the smiling man. 'What?'

'I ain't paid you yet, friend!'

'Plenty time for money!'

'I like to settle my debts up front!' Sunset reached into his pants pocket and withdrew some folded money. He peeled off three fifty-dollar bills and gave them to Krugar. 'For the pack-horse, the water and the gun!'

The larger man smiled. 'This too much!'

'It ain't nearly enough!'

'You mighty good man!' Krugar said.

Johnny Sunset moved towards his mount and ran a gloved hand along its black coat. The stallion nodded and turned to look at its master. The bounty hunter picked up the blanket from the sand and placed it upon the animal's back. He then lifted up his saddle and threw it on top of the tall horse. As Sunset leaned under the horse's belly and pulled the cinch strap towards him he glanced over his shoulder at the large happy figure and whispered.

'You really don't know me very well!'

8

Deadman's Draw was indeed a strange, unholy place. Even coyotes did not raise their baying heads to the moon here. If there was anything living it remained silent and unseen by the eyes of the five riders who journeyed further and further into its dangerous heart. The blistering heat of the day had been replaced by the freezing temperatures of nightfall. Yet the weary men with their bags full of money had not faltered in their quest. Now with the eerie blue moon above them, they had reached their destination at last.

The slight rise of blackened rocks amid the rolling virgin sand dunes which seemed to go on for ever in each direction gave no clue to the secret it marked far below the surface. Yet the accidental discovery had proved to be Carver's salvation several times before.

Carver reined in. His eyes studied the entire horizon as if knowing that this time someone would follow. This time he and his gang would not escape. It seemed ridiculous even to the outlaw himself, yet the fear was real. He had always felt that every man was given only so much good luck and there would come a time when it had to run out. Like the sand inside an hourglass it had to run out eventually. His men drew rein around him and watched Carver like children watch their father.

Sensing the eyes burning into his soul, Moss Carver inhaled long and hard. His dry nostrils could smell the water which was now within walking distance. Carver dismounted and pulled the collar of his jacket up to protect his neck from the coldness which swept unhindered across the desolation.

'C'mon, boys! Follow me!' The outlaw leader grabbed hold of his horse's bridle and began the steep descent into the blackness between the rocks.

'There's a storm brewing, Moss!'

Fargo noted as he and the rest of the men eased themselves off their horses' backs.

'Ain't gonna trouble us none!' Carver replied. 'Not where we're going! C'mon!'

The sound of water filled Carver's ears. It was a sweet sound, like music to a man who had felt every last drop of his body's sweat evaporate beneath the desert sun.

Each of the horsemen again did as he was ordered. Now they too could smell the scent of the precious liquid. In this barren landscape, water was more valuable even than gold nuggets. Without it the wealthiest of men would die just as easily as a pauper.

The sandy trail led steeply down into a place which none of them could make out clearly. Not even the illumination of the bright moon high above them could find its way into the depths of this strange place.

Muller was close behind Carver. His younger eyes vainly tried to see the water they could all hear.

'How far is it, Moss?'

Carver glanced over his shoulder. 'Can't you recall the last couple of times we was here, Sol?'

'Nope!' the outlaw admitted. 'I recall we were all a tad drunk when we followed you out here from the rich pickings back at San Angelo!'

'Ain't far!' Carver said.

'Where's the torches, Moss?' English called out. His words echoed all around them. 'I recall torches! You had a whole bunch of them spaced out! Where are they?'

Carver did not reply. He stopped and ventured close to the cave wall on his right. His free hand found a match in his jacket pockets. His thumbnail ran across its tip. The flickering light revealed a torch jutting out of the wall from a natural crack in its rugged surface. Carver touched the flame to the oily rag wrapped around the top of the wooden stake. Suddenly the warm light was everywhere.

'I see another one about twenty feet

down there!' Davis said excitedly.

Carver tossed the blackened match away, reached up and pulled the torch from its resting place. He held it high, then began walking once more.

'I'll light them all up and each of you boys take one!' Carver said firmly.

The ground beneath their high-heeled boots grew even steeper and more slippery. The walking men led their horses down towards the place they knew was getting closer with every passing beat of their rancid hearts.

As Carver passed each torch mounted on the cave walls he touched its top with the flames of his own torch. Light began to spread further and further down the weird trail. As ordered each man took one and continued into the chasm. The light grew greater with each additional torch but still they were unable to see the fast-flowing water they could all hear so distinctly.

'How many other folks know of this place, Moss?' Fargo asked.

'Just us!' Carver said as his eyes were

greeted by the sight of the dark, fresh water flowing below them.

'Injuns gotta know about this place!' Shale Davis disagreed.

Carver gave a short chuckle. 'There ain't no damn Injuns around here no more, you idiot!'

'How come?' Muller wondered aloud.

'White folks and Mexicans killed the whole stinking bunch of them years back!' Carver snorted. 'It's called progress back East!'

'I bet there's still a few Apaches around here someplace!' Fargo snorted. 'Apaches are sneaky, y'know?'

The men went silent for the next seemingly endless minute until Carver stopped walking and they too could all see the underground river.

The five torches lit up the area with their uncanny flickering light. Carver's gang looked up at the vaulted cave ceiling which stood at least thirty feet above their heads. None of them knew it but they were looking at the remnant of a once powerful river that had at one time filled the vast expanse around them. Now the underground river barely filled half the tunnel floor and seemed to be getting shallower each time they reached this place. The only good fortune for the outlaws was that the dry banks to either side of the ice-cold water made it possible to travel the tunnel in its entirety. Carver looked to his right and rubbed his neck. The light from the torches danced upon the water yet only reached a score of yards from where they all stood. He knew that the cave tunnel stretched halfway along the length of the infamous Deadman's Draw far above. Never more than forty feet beneath the arid ground, it allowed men to survive the brutal heat and cut their journey in half. Three times he had journeyed this way and led his men to the safety of the lush plains beyond.

Carver turned and looked at his men. They were dragging the edge of the river for the barrels of beer they had left in this strange place a year earlier. He allowed his mount to walk to the river and start drinking with the other horses, then he checked his weaponry nervously.

Hope English limped towards the thoughtful Carver and removed his battered hat. He could see the cans of food they had stockpiled twelve months before, stacked by the wall. But it was not food he wanted but answers.

'You gonna let me quit, Moss?'

Carver did not look up. He stood in the light of the torches which his men had rammed into the damp ground and sighed as his fingers ensured that every chamber of his guns was loaded with fresh bullets.

English edged even closer. 'I'm spent, Moss! Spent like a mustang who bin run into the ground! I ain't no good for you or the boys no more! Let me hang up my guns when we gets out on the other side of the canyon!'

'We got cans of beans and peaches over yonder, Hope!' Carver said slowly before he slid his weapons back into their holsters.

ere headed, for they had followed the oof-tracks of the man they sought to his place.

There was vengeance in their heartless souls. It burned like acid in their innards. It was a fire which could only be doused by the blood of the bounty hunter they trailed. Skeet and Will Bower had already discovered back at San Carlos that their brothers were dead. They had seen the stiffening corpses with the bullet holes in them on the undertaker's slab. Both riders had been delayed in their meeting with their siblings back at the border town and now burned with fiery rods of retribution.

They had learned the truth about the fate of Rufe and Lane from the sheriff back there. It had taken less than ten minutes of expertly executed torture for the lawman to spill the beans.

After killing the lawman the outlaws had headed on out for Silver City. Both had the name of Johnny Sunset branded into their memories. He had killed their closest kin and that was

'I gotta quit!' English growled in a desperate tone designed for the ears of only one man. 'Look at me for God's sake! I'm rusted up!'

Carver looked into the eyes before him. 'Damn it all! I need you, Hope! You and me bin together the longest time! We fought shoulder to shoulder long before these other runts even knew there was a war on! You can't leave me with this bunch of snot-nosed kids!'

English placed a hand on the outlaw's shoulder. 'Look at them, Moss! They ain't kids no more! They're old like we are! Maybe not as old but this life has aged the lot of us! All the money we've stolen don't amount to a hill of beans to any of us! This life ages a man, Moss! Look at them!'

Carver's eyes darted to the other three as they cracked the beer barrel open and started to fill their canteens with its ice-cold contents. For the first time for years he could actually see them as they really were. They were as English had said. Young old men. His jaw dropped open.

'Sweet Lord!' he muttered.

'We all gotta settle down!' English whispered. 'Settle down and enjoy all the money we've collected over the last couple of years! Before it's too damn late!'

Carver pulled away from his old friend. He began clapping his hands. The sound echoed all around them. 'C'mon, boys! The vittles are over here waiting to be eaten!'

English shook his weary head and looked down at the ground.

Carver had heard his own fears put into words by his oldest comrade and it chilled him. He glanced at English and then felt the hairs on the back of his neck rise.

'What's wrong, Moss?' Davis wondered aloud.

Carver inhaled. 'Nothing!' he lied.

9

Midnight covered the borderland in cloak of darkness. Yet the glowing numerous coal-tar lanterns defied natur and beckoned to all seeking a port of cal in an otherwise barren ocean of sand and sagebrush. The street lights of Silver City had drawn many things from out on the vast range over the years, yet the pair of horsemen who approached the outskirts of the remote town were probably the most dangerous. Both men rode with their heads lowered out of the moonlit range but their eyes were aimed straight ahead at the winding streets, which appeared to be virtually deserted. The weathered signpost with the name of the remote settlement painted upon its flaking surface was ignored by both horsemen as they tapped their spurs again and again into the already bloody flanks of their mounts. They knew exactly where they something for which the bounty hunter would have to pay the ultimate price. Not that either of the riders had actually liked their brothers but where they came from there was a code. They were simply following that code and the man known as Sunset.

The riders looked all around them as they began to navigate through the streets which would eventually lead them to the sheriff's office. Unlike most outlaws the Bower brothers had never feared the law. They had never doubted their own abilities. So far two of the brothers had died because of that blind arrogance.

Skeet Bower raised his gun arm and pointed his trigger finger along the street. Will nodded and pulled his reins to his left towards the sign nailed to the porch overhang.

The men hauled back on their long leathers.

They stared up at the sign, then lowered their cruel eyes and glared at the light coming from within the sheriff's office.

Skeet dismounted first. He looped his reins around the hitching rail and secured it as his brother dropped down to the ground and copied his actions.

'Another fat 'un by the looks of it, brother!' Skeet said in a hoarse whisper as his eyes burned through the glass pane at the seated lawman.

'We gonna kill this critter, Skeet?'

The elder Bower brother gave a slow nod. 'Yep! If'n he don't tell where the famous Sunset Kid is holed up!'

'I reckon we ought to kill him even if he tells us, Skeet!'

The elder brother nodded. 'You might be right there!'

Their spurs rang out as they stepped up on to the boardwalk outside the office. Skeet turned the doorknob and pushed the door inwards.

Lou Favor glanced up from behind his desk. For a moment he did not feel troubled. Yet when Will Bower leaned across the stack of Wanted posters and dragged the lawman out of his chair, Favor realized something was wrong.

'W . . . what you want?' Favor yelped.

Will Bower did not release his grip until the overweight sheriff was balancing on the very edge of his desk. Then the outlaw let go. Favor crashed hard into the boards. He felt his left collar bone snap like a dried twig.

'Aaaagh!' The sheriff cried out.

Skeet Bower closed the door and stared out at the quiet street bathed in lantern light. He locked the door and then lashed out with his right boot. The sheriff felt himself being kicked halfway across the office. Even his ample covering of flesh could not protect his ribs from the pointed tip of the boot.

Again he grunted in agony.

'Where's Sunset?' the older brother snarled. 'We come looking for a stinking bounty hunter who calls himself Johnny Sunset or the Sunset Kid! He killed our brothers! Where is he?'

Favor tried to get up but it was impossible. Not with Will Bower standing on both his hands. The lawman looked up into each of the cruel twisted faces.

'Who are you?' Favor managed to ask.

'Answer the damn question, fatman!' Skeet repeated. 'Where's the bastard who killed our brothers? We was told that he was headed here to collect his blood money! Where is he? He bought himself some whores or is he just lording it up in some saloon?'

'He's gone!' The sheriff coughed and saw blood spatter from his mouth on to the floor beside his head.

Will Bower leaned forward until his weight was fully on his boots. The sound of knuckles cracking in the sheriff's hands filled the room.

'Aaagh! Stop! For God's sake! Stop!'

Skeet paced around the prostrate man and his brother. 'Gone? Where'd he go? We sure didn't pass him out on the trail!'

'He was here!' Favor coughed desperately. 'But he lit on out after some desperadoes!'

Will Bower leaned over and spat a lump of goo into the face of the sheriff. 'How much did he make off my brothers' hides?'

Terror filled the lawman. 'He didn't collect a red cent!'

Skeet Bower drew in a breath and then swung his right boot into the guts of the man his brother had pinned to the floor. Favor buckled and then cried out in agony. The elder of the brothers gave out a wry smile.

'This 'un is as soft as the one back at San Carlos, Will!'

'This 'un is quite a lot fatter than most!' Will Bower walked to the window and stared out. If there were any people out at this time of the night, he sure could not see any of them. He pulled the blind down and looked back at the man on the floor as Skeet kicked Favor again. 'Why don't we just kill the bastard and go on after Sunset, Skeet?'

Favor spat out a mouthful of blood. 'I'm telling the truth! We had our bank robbed and Sunset went on out after the outlaws who done it! He couldn't collect his reward money and that made him kinda ornery!'

Skeet bent over and looked hard into the watery eyes of the man they had virtually crippled. 'You gonna pay him for the bounty on this other bunch if he comes back?'

'Who are you?' Favor gasped.

'Who are we?' Skeet growled as if angered by the lack of recognition. 'We are what's left of the Bower brothers!'

'Ain't ever heard of you!' the sheriff defiantly lied.

The brothers looked at one another.

'Where did he go?' Will shouted down at the lawman. 'Which direction did Sunset take?'

'South-east!' Favor waved an arm as though pointing to the far side of town. He managed to get up on to his knees, then he glanced at the men who stood between himself and his holstered gun hanging from his hat rack. Then through his tears he saw his broken hands and spat blood at the floor. Even if he had his seldom-used gun he knew he could not fire it. 'He rode on out past the livery!'

'I gotta quit!' English growled in a desperate tone designed for the ears of only one man. 'Look at me for God's sake! I'm rusted up!'

Carver looked into the eyes before him. 'Damn it all! I need you, Hope! You and me bin together the longest time! We fought shoulder to shoulder long before these other runts even knew there was a war on! You can't leave me with this bunch of snot-nosed kids!'

English placed a hand on the outlaw's shoulder. 'Look at them, Moss! They ain't kids no more! They're old like we are! Maybe not as old but this life has aged the lot of us! All the money we've stolen don't amount to a hill of beans to any of us! This life ages a man, Moss! Look at them!'

Carver's eyes darted to the other three as they cracked the beer barrel open and started to fill their canteens with its ice-cold contents. For the first time for years he could actually see them as they really were. They were as English had said. Young old men. His jaw dropped open.

'Sweet Lord!' he muttered.

'We all gotta settle down!' English whispered. 'Settle down and enjoy all the money we've collected over the last couple of years! Before it's too damn late!'

Carver pulled away from his old friend. He began clapping his hands. The sound echoed all around them. 'C'mon, boys! The vittles are over here waiting to be eaten!'

English shook his weary head and looked down at the ground.

Carver had heard his own fears put into words by his oldest comrade and it chilled him. He glanced at English and then felt the hairs on the back of his neck rise.

'What's wrong, Moss?' Davis wondered aloud.

Carver inhaled. 'Nothing!' he lied.

9

Midnight covered the borderland in its cloak of darkness. Yet the glowing of numerous coal-tar lanterns defied nature and beckoned to all seeking a port of call in an otherwise barren ocean of sand and sagebrush. The street lights of Silver City had drawn many things from out on the vast range over the years, yet the pair of horsemen who approached the outskirts of the remote town were probably the most dangerous. Both men rode with their heads lowered out of the moonlit range but their eyes were aimed straight ahead at the winding streets, which appeared to be virtually deserted. The weathered signpost with the name of the remote settlement painted upon its flaking surface was ignored by both horsemen as they tapped their spurs again and again into the already bloody flanks of their mounts. They knew exactly where they were headed, for they had followed the hoof-tracks of the man they sought to this place.

There was vengeance in their heartless souls. It burned like acid in their innards. It was a fire which could only be doused by the blood of the bounty hunter they trailed. Skeet and Will Bower had already discovered back at San Carlos that their brothers were dead. They had seen the stiffening corpses with the bullet holes in them on the undertaker's slab. Both riders had been delayed in their meeting with their siblings back at the border town and now burned with fiery rods of retribution.

They had learned the truth about the fate of Rufe and Lane from the sheriff back there. It had taken less than ten minutes of expertly executed torture for the lawman to spill the beans.

After killing the lawman the outlaws had headed on out for Silver City. Both had the name of Johnny Sunset branded into their memories. He had killed their closest kin and that was something for which the bounty hunter would have to pay the ultimate price. Not that either of the riders had actually liked their brothers but where they came from there was a code. They were simply following that code and the man known as Sunset.

The riders looked all around them as they began to navigate through the streets which would eventually lead them to the sheriff's office. Unlike most outlaws the Bower brothers had never feared the law. They had never doubted their own abilities. So far two of the brothers had died because of that blind arrogance.

Skeet Bower raised his gun arm and pointed his trigger finger along the street. Will nodded and pulled his reins to his left towards the sign nailed to the porch overhang.

The men hauled back on their long leathers.

They stared up at the sign, then lowered their cruel eyes and glared at the light coming from within the sheriff's office.

Skeet dismounted first. He looped his reins around the hitching rail and secured it as his brother dropped down to the ground and copied his actions.

'Another fat 'un by the looks of it, brother!' Skeet said in a hoarse whisper as his eyes burned through the glass pane at the seated lawman.

'We gonna kill this critter, Skeet?'

The elder Bower brother gave a slow nod. 'Yep! If'n he don't tell where the famous Sunset Kid is holed up!'

'I reckon we ought to kill him even if he tells us, Skeet!'

The elder brother nodded. 'You might be right there!'

Their spurs rang out as they stepped up on to the boardwalk outside the office. Skeet turned the doorknob and pushed the door inwards.

Lou Favor glanced up from behind his desk. For a moment he did not feel troubled. Yet when Will Bower leaned across the stack of Wanted posters and dragged the lawman out of his chair, Favor realized something was wrong.

'W . . . what you want?' Favor yelped.

Will Bower did not release his grip until the overweight sheriff was balancing on the very edge of his desk. Then the outlaw let go. Favor crashed hard into the boards. He felt his left collar bone snap like a dried twig.

'Aaaagh!' The sheriff cried out.

Skeet Bower closed the door and stared out at the quiet street bathed in lantern light. He locked the door and then lashed out with his right boot. The sheriff felt himself being kicked halfway across the office. Even his ample covering of flesh could not protect his ribs from the pointed tip of the boot.

Again he grunted in agony.

'Where's Sunset?' the older brother snarled. 'We come looking for a stinking bounty hunter who calls himself Johnny Sunset or the Sunset Kid! He killed our brothers! Where is he?'

Favor tried to get up but it was impossible. Not with Will Bower standing on both his hands. The lawman looked up into each of the cruel twisted faces.

'Who are you?' Favor managed to ask.

'Answer the damn question, fatman!' Skeet repeated. 'Where's the bastard who killed our brothers? We was told that he was headed here to collect his blood money! Where is he? He bought himself some whores or is he just lording it up in some saloon?'

'He's gone!' The sheriff coughed and saw blood spatter from his mouth on to the floor beside his head.

Will Bower leaned forward until his weight was fully on his boots. The sound of knuckles cracking in the sheriff's hands filled the room.

'Aaagh! Stop! For God's sake! Stop!'

Skeet paced around the prostrate man and his brother. 'Gone? Where'd he go? We sure didn't pass him out on the trail!'

'He was here!' Favor coughed desperately. 'But he lit on out after some desperadoes!'

Will Bower leaned over and spat a lump of goo into the face of the sheriff. 'How much did he make off my brothers' hides?'

Terror filled the lawman. 'He didn't collect a red cent!'

Skeet Bower drew in a breath and then swung his right boot into the guts of the man his brother had pinned to the floor. Favor buckled and then cried out in agony. The elder of the brothers gave out a wry smile.

'This 'un is as soft as the one back at San Carlos, Will!'

'This 'un is quite a lot fatter than most!' Will Bower walked to the window and stared out. If there were any people out at this time of the night, he sure could not see any of them. He pulled the blind down and looked back at the man on the floor as Skeet kicked Favor again. 'Why don't we just kill the bastard and go on after Sunset, Skeet?'

Favor spat out a mouthful of blood. 'I'm telling the truth! We had our bank robbed and Sunset went on out after the outlaws who done it! He couldn't collect his reward money and that made him kinda ornery!'

Skeet bent over and looked hard into the watery eyes of the man they had virtually crippled. 'You gonna pay him for the bounty on this other bunch if he comes back?'

'Who are you?' Favor gasped.

'Who are we?' Skeet growled as if angered by the lack of recognition. 'We are what's left of the Bower brothers!'

'Ain't ever heard of you!' the sheriff defiantly lied.

The brothers looked at one another.

'Where did he go?' Will shouted down at the lawman. 'Which direction did Sunset take?'

'South-east!' Favor waved an arm as though pointing to the far side of town. He managed to get up on to his knees, then he glanced at the men who stood between himself and his holstered gun hanging from his hat rack. Then through his tears he saw his broken hands and spat blood at the floor. Even if he had his seldom-used gun he knew he could not fire it. 'He rode on out past the livery!'

'That's in the direction of the desert, ain't it?' Skeet Bower asked his sibling. 'Deadman's Draw is between here and the next town! Nobody would head that way!'

Will nodded. 'He must be loco!'

'The Sunset Kid ain't loco!' Favor said through bloody teeth. 'But you sure must be if'n you're thinking of tangling with him, sonny!'

Skeet rested his right hand on the grip of one of his guns and looked at his brother. 'Sunset ain't loco, he's simply trailing the bastards who robbed the bank! It's them that must be real dumb! Everyone knows that there ain't nothing that can live out there in that desert!'

'We still gonna follow?' Will asked.

'Follow him and get yourselves killed!' the sheriff snarled.

Skeet drew one of his guns and cocked its hammer. He stared down its blue steel barrel at the bloody face of the man on his knees and smiled. He then squeezed the trigger. The deafening sound of the shot echoed all around the office as gore splattered across the walls behind the lifeless body. What was left of Favor fell in a crumpled heap.

'You bet, brother! We're still gonna chase and catch that *hombre* and make him pay for killing our kinfolk!'

Will watched as Skeet holstered his smoking gun. 'Do you think this lawman might be right to how good Sunset is, Skeet?'

'Nope! He just got lucky with Rufe and Lane!'

'And the desert?'

'I ain't scared of sand, brother!'

Will Bower rubbed his hands together gleefully. 'It's my turn to kill the Sunset Kid, Skeet! When we catches up with him I wanna kill him!'

'You'll have to beat me to the draw, brother!'

They unlocked the office door and marched out on to the boardwalk. Gunsmoke trailed out into the cold night air after them but neither outlaw noticed. All they had on their minds was revenge. They pulled their reins free, mounted, spun the animals round and spurred.

The Bower brothers thundered through the streets of Silver City at breakneck pace.

Johnny Sunset did not know it but now there were outlaws on his trail.

The hunter was also the hunted.

10

Most deserts were designed to kill. Kill by a thousand different methods. Even without the deadly lizards and the poisonous snakes it could kill. The unimaginable heat of the day and the freezing cold of night were both designed to kill. Men were not designed to cope with either yet since time first began they braved the elements and defied the dangers. Some men were drawn to peril the way moths could not resist a naked flame. Yet the infamous bounty hunter was not a man who stood up against the elements foolishly or for no reason. He had the scent of his prey in his nostrils and it was only their trail which had brought him to this place. He wanted the money on their heads and he followed wherever it led.

For hours Sunset had felt the cold

gnawing into his bones as he had followed the well-defined hoof-tracks left by the Carver gang's horses. Now as he drew back on his reins and stopped the powerful stallion beneath him he realized that it was becoming warmer. That meant only one thing. It would soon be sunup.

He glanced back at the sturdy packhorse laden down with leather bags filled with water. The bounty hunter raised his right leg, looped it over the neck of his stallion and slid down to the sand. The blue light cast down from the moon was as good as the midday sun for the keen eyes of the man who tracked men for a living. He had managed to follow their trail to this remote place but now the canvas of sand was blank. The steady breeze which came from the canyon ahead had obliterated all the hoof-tracks left by Carver and his gang.

'Damn it all!' Sunset muttered as he walked along the length of his black mount until he reached the waterbags tied to the packhorse. He checked the leather lace bindings before moving back to the head of his prized mount. 'That's all we need! Of all times to lose their damn trail!'

The breeze was slow but steady. He could feel its fine grains cutting into his face and taste the sand in his mouth. He spat and then pulled the brim of his hat down to shield his eyes. The tall lean figure rested the knuckles of his right hand on the newly made gun and stared at the daunting apparition.

'So that's Deadman's Draw!' Sunset said, searching the horizon for an alternative route southeast. If there was one he sure could not see it. If a man was starting from where he stood there was just one choice and that was to head into the jaws of Hell, he thought. 'Don't look so fearsome in the moonlight! But then looks can be kinda deceptive!'

The words had no sooner left his lips than he saw the bones of an animal close to where he stood. Whatever it was, they had been picked clean. A bead of sweat trailed down from his hatband and traced his jaw.

Johnny Sunset turned to his horse and spat again. 'That canyon and its rockfaces look no more dangerous than all the others we've faced, horse, but I ain't fooled! I knows that men don't last too long in there, boy! Even wild mustangs that can live off fresh air can't outwit that place! We gotta be smart if'n we want to outwit that inferno!'

His long slim legs paced a wide circle around the two animals as he wondered whether he could find the men he sought before being forced to enter Deadman's Draw. The high walls of rock which flanked the canyon appeared to trail off for ever in both directions. Sunset was seldom afraid of anything but the thought of getting into trouble in a place where nothing appeared capable of surviving made him anxious.

Again his eyes studied the sand. The trail left by the gang of outlaws ended a few feet from where his boots sank into the soft sand. He raised a hand and tried to work out the direction the hoof-marks had been heading before being blown away. He turned and screwed up his eyes.

'I figure they went thataway, horse!' Sunset said pointing a gloved finger. 'What in tarnation could be out there? Is there something I can't see?'

He rubbed his face deep in thought. 'There had to be some reason that Carver and his boys went over yonder! Maybe they didn't head straight into Deadman's Draw at all! Carver ain't dumb! Why would he? But then again, that varmint was a soldier who wore the grey and he's tough! Men like him don't live their lives by the rules like ordinary folks!'

The stallion snorted. It turned its head and looked at its master. Sunset returned the look.

'I ain't talking to myself, horse! I'm talking to you!'

The black stallion looked away and snorted again. Sunset walked back to the packhorse and pulled one of the cold damp bags free. Using his Stetson as a bowl he watered both animals as his mind raced for answers.

Then, as Sunset returned the bag to the packanimal's back he noticed the glow along the horizon. The stars were beginning to disappear as the sun came close to rising.

'Gonna be sunup soon! We have to find us some place to shelter before that sun gets high! We'll roast up like a Thanksgiving turkey on a spit otherwise!'

Johnny Sunset pushed his boot into his stirrup, pulled himself atop the high-shouldered horse and gathered up his reins. He stood in his stirrups and balanced as he again surveyed the horizon ahead of him, looking for refuge. Then, just when he thought that there was nowhere to keep the new day's rays off himself and his animals, he spotted a slight rise to his right. The very direction where he had thought Carver's trail was headed.

Johnny Sunset teased his reins, turned the stallion and squinted even harder.

The black rocks were at least three miles away. He wondered whether they were as big as they looked and if so would they offer enough shade to protect him?

For the first time since he had set out from Silver City, Sunset had no thought of the men he pursued or how much bounty they carried on their heads. All Sunset could think of now was getting to a place where there might be shade enough to allow him and his animals to survive.

The bounty hunter raised his reins and whipped the shoulders of the stallion. The animal beneath his saddle responded as it always responded and began to plough through the sandy terrain with the packhorse close behind.

Now it was a race against time.

How long would it take for the merciless sun to rise?

Did he have enough time to reach the black rocks?

Even if he did, would it be a safe haven or just another place where flesh was bleached off the bones of those who had also ventured into this dangerous place?

A lot of questions.

Not a single answer.

As the rider urged his mount on Johnny Sunset felt the air becoming warmer. He could see the mist rising from the sand all around him as the heat of day banished the freezing cold of night. A sickening fog surrounded them on all sides. The horseman had to recall exactly where they had seen the rise of rocks and aim his mount accordingly. The mist appeared to be getting even thicker the further they galloped.

The beautiful stallion had barely covered a half-mile when the blinding sun appeared over the desolate horizon. Its light swept like a tidal wave over everything before it. With the light came the heat.

Merciless heat.

Sunset glanced briefly at the blinding orb. It was like having branding-irons thrust into his eyes. Then the sun itself also disappeared behind the fog which its heat had created. But even masked by the evaporation of untold acres of icy dew it still burned the side of the rider's face.

A frightening thought entered Sunset's mind. If it was this hot at sunup, what would it be like at high noon? He continued to whip the shoulders of his muscular mount.

The sand was getting softer beneath the pounding hoofs of his mount. The stallion's strength was beginning to ebb.

The Sunset Kid began to wonder whether they would ever manage to reach their goal.

11

Moss Carver had tried to sleep but it had proved impossible as his men drank and ate their fill of the provisions he had laid down on their previous visit to the sanctuary carved out of solid rock by nature over an untold number of years. Even after they had fallen asleep Carver had still been unable to close his own eyes. The man who had always prided himself on his cold-blooded attitude to everything had found that now he was beginning to realize that he too was mortal.

But it was not fear that haunted him. It was the nightmares that always haunted men of his breed. The faces of so many of his fellow soldiers were burned into his memory. He had seen so much carnage in his short lifetime. Too much carnage. Silver City had been the first time since the end of the war that death had come close to his dwindling band.

The torches still burned and sent their light dancing across the fast-flowing underground waterway. Carver stood and moved to the river's edge and stared into its blackness. He looked to his left and wondered what lay in that direction. Where did the river go? He had only ever gone to their right and come out halfway along the canyon deep in the depths of Deadman's Draw.

Survival had always been something which Carver had been blessed with. His gut instincts had always alerted him to the dangers others could not even imagine. So it was now. Something deep inside him burned as hot as their torches. Something was warning him that they were not free and clear this time.

There had been nobody trailing them out into the desert, he kept telling himself, yet his innards told him another tale. He knew that death was riding after them.

Death had travelled with them for years but had never turned on them. His mind thought of Vin Egan lying there on the porch of the bank with a hole through his guts. Eighteen inches to the left and it would have been him that had been cut in half and not Egan. Carver widened his fingers and ran them through his sweat-soaked hair.

He turned and looked at the snoring men who had managed to finish every last drop of the beer and consume more than half of the canned goods.

But they were not all snoring.

Hope English was propped up against the wall of the cave with eyes wide open. Constant pain had a way of keeping men awake as easily as haunting thoughts. The torchlight illuminated his tortured features.

Carver walked back to his old friend.

'You can't sleep either?' English commented.

'Nope!'

'I'm in pain, Moss!' English said bluntly. 'What's your damn excuse?'

111

Carver looked up the steep tunnel down which they had journeyed hours earlier and rubbed his neck. His eyes darted from the sleeping outlaws to the resting horses, and then back to the man on the ground at his feet.

'I got me a bad feeling about this, Hope!'

English gave a slow nod. 'I figured as much by the way you bin acting! What's eating you?'

Carver inhaled deeply. 'I got me a feeling that we ain't gonna get away this time!'

'You got doubts? You never got doubts, Moss!'

'I know it don't make no sense!' Carver licked his lips but there was no spittle. 'We got clean away with the bank money. Not a hint of anyone on our trail and we're only hours away from getting on the far side of the canyon and freedom. We'll be south of the border before the day is out and yet I got me something gnawing at my craw, Hope. I can't figure it.'

English nodded again. 'You can see your own tombstone at last, Moss. Most men die coz they can see themselves that way but you never saw nothing but victory. Every battle we fought you led the way. You never seen no marker with your name on it and that's why you never even got a scratch. Now you realize that death is out there waiting for you just like every, other stupid bastard who ever drew air into his lungs.'

Carver looked away. 'Do you believe in omens, Hope?'

'Sure do.'

Carver punched his clenched fist into the palm of his left hand and snorted.

'I feel that we got us company up there.'

English held out a hand and was helped to his feet by the man who had never once failed to get the better of odds which were often stacked against them. His wrinkled eyes stared hard into Carver's face.

'But you looked hard and long back

at our tracks, Moss. You never seen nobody following.'

'I didn't see him but I feel him, Hope! He's coming after us and he's not like the others who tried. This 'un is good.'

English leaned closer. 'Who?'

'Who? You ask who? Whatever they call him I reckon his real handle is Death! I can feel him in my guts, Hope. Death is on our trail and we gotta get him before he gets us!'

'Death?' English swallowed hard. He could not hide the troubled expression from his friend. 'Death ain't a living breathing critter like us, boy! Death's not a man!'

Carver nodded. 'You care to bet on that, Hope? You care to wager your share of our loot that I'm wrong?'

English smiled. 'I learned long ago never to bet with a varmint as lucky as you, Moss.'

Carver stepped over to their stacked saddles and dragged two Winchesters from their scabbards. He tossed one to

English, then looked up the steep tunnel they had descended to reach this cool sanctuary. He pushed the hand-guard down and then drew it back up again. The rifle was cocked and readied.

'Let's go up there and take us a look, Hope.' Carver said.

'A look at what, Moss?' English primed his own weapon.

'Let's go see what Death looks like!'

The two outlaws left their three companions sleeping off their drink and began the journey up to the surface. They could see the blue sky and, after a dozen paces, they could also feel the desert heat.

12

The wall of damp mist felt good to the horseman as he whipped the shoulders of his trusty mount and led the heavily laden packhorse towards the rocky outcrop. Yet Johnny Sunset knew full well that in a few more minutes the cool vapour would be nothing more than a memory. The blistering sun was already casting its deadly heat across the vast expanse of sand as the bounty hunter charged on towards his distant goal. Then as the fog lifted for a brief few seconds ahead of the black stallion's nose, Sunset saw them.

Two shapes, which Sunset knew could only be men, moved behind the black rocks. The sun caught the long metal barrels of their carbines and flashed its warning light like a beacon. Sunset hauled back on his reins and brought the sturdy animal beneath his saddle to a violent halt.

The new day was less than ten minutes old when the pair of hardened outlaws reached the rise of black rocks which marked the entrance to the secret tunnel. To men who had spent most of the night beside the cool subterranean river the heat was overwhelming. Mist encircled them as the sun dragged every ounce of the night's moisture out of the yellow sand.

English rested a hand on the rocks and steadied himself when Carver swung on his heels, raised the rifle to his shoulder and cried out.

'There he is!' Carver screamed in a way that his pal recalled from their days together on the battlefields.

The older man blinked hard, then turned and looked to where his cohort was aiming the Winchester's long barrel. Then he too saw the strange apparition through the swirling mist of vapour.

English felt his jaw drop. 'Huh?'

'I told you,' Carver proclaimed. His

finger jerked the trigger and the rifle spewed out a plume of hot fire and smoke.

Sunset used the fog like a shield against the deadly bullet which hurtled towards him. He dragged the long leathers to his right and managed to turn the powerful stallion before the outlaw could cock his rifle a second time.

The bounty hunter swung his horse round until it was facing its own hoof-tracks, with its back to the rifleman. He then spurred hard and galloped back into the safety of the dense mist.

Another rod of lead lightning passed within a yard of him as he swiftly dropped from his saddle. Sunset slapped the rump of his stallion and watched the animal lead the packhorse off deeper into the cover of the fog. He knew the stallion would return at the sound of just one whistle.

Sunset dropped on to one knee and stared hard through the moving whirl-pool of evaporating dew. Another shot rang out and then another. Both bullets went high over him. He knew that the man with the Winchester could not see him. He also knew that neither of his guns could match the rifle for range. Somehow he had to get closer if he were to have any chance of hitting his target before he himself were hit.

A coward would have dug a hole in the sand and hidden but Sunset was no coward. His eyes narrowed as his mind raced for a solution.

Behind the rocks, Carver cranked the mechanism of the Winchester again and blasted another bullet into the swirling wall of moisture.

'Death rides a black horse, Hope!' Carver announced.

English scrambled to the side of his ranting pal and grabbed the man's shoulder. Carver's eyes darted to his companion.

'Did you see him, Hope?' Carver asked frantically. 'Did you see the bastard?'

'I seen him, Moss,' English nodded.

'I told you he was after us, Hope.' Carver unleashed another shot and pushed the guard of his rifle back down. The spent casing flew over English's elbow before Carver hauled the guard up again. 'I told you Death was coming! You seen him! My innards ain't never bin wrong. Never!'

English watched as his pal squeezed the trigger once more. The deafening sound made the older man wince as he shook Carver's shoulder again.

'Listen to me, Moss!'

Carver lowered the rifle. 'What?'

'Let's get back down to the boys and start on through the tunnel,' English implored. 'He's pinned down out there! You scared him and he'll probably stay belly down for hours. We can use that time to our advantage.'

'I gotta kill him!' Carver snapped. 'Kill him before he kills us, Hope! You seen him! He's real! Death is real!'

'I seen a rider!' English pressed his lips against the ear of the wide-eyed man. 'A rider, Moss. We don't know that he's after us.'

'He's after us!' Carver insisted. 'Why

would anyone be out here if he ain't on our trail?'

English began to pull the man away from the rocks and towards the tunnel once more.

'Maybe he's loco. Maybe he's just lost.'

Carver dug his boots into the sand and pushed the rifle barrel into English's ample belly. 'I have to finish this! Don't try and stop me or I'll have to finish you!'

Hope English released his grip. 'OK. Kill me. You'd be doing me a favour, Moss! Go on! Shoot!'

Carver shook his head and regained his wits. He turned the rifle away from English and moved back to the rocks. He leaned down and rested the long barrel on the top of the rocks.

'OK. It was just a rider. But he's after us, Hope. That I'm certain about!'

English heard the sound of their three fellow outlaws rushing up the tunnel slope towards them. Their spurs echoed.

'The boys are coming, Moss.'

Carver did not reply. He lay with one eye closed whilst the other looked along the length of the rifle barrel through its sights.

'When the mist rises I'm gonna put a bullet right between his eyes! Whoever he is, I'm gonna kill him!'

Fargo led Muller and Davis into the brilliant sunshine. They each held their six-shooters in their hands and stared at their fellow outlaws in bewildered silence.

English waved them back. 'Get back down there and get the horses readied, boys. We'll be heading on out along the tunnel in a few minutes.'

Carver glanced at English as the three other men turned and ran back down into the cool of their underground sanctuary. His face was burning with fury.

'I give the orders around here, Hope! Not you! Me!'

English hobbled back to the side of his partner in crime. He eased himself down and cocked his own rifle. He rested it on top of the rocks, spat into his hand and wet its sights with thumb and fingers.

'You get down there with the boys, Moss.' English said firmly. 'I'll wait for the mist to rise. I'll kill him for you.'

Carver stared hard into English's face. It was a face etched by unceasing pain. 'I wanna kill him!'

'You get down there and lead them boys to safety!' the older man drawled. 'If you're smart you'll use some of the dynamite I know you got in your saddle-bags and blow up the tunnel so nobody can trail you.'

'What about you?'

'Like I bin telling you, I'm finished!' English looked at the man who had led him and the others for so long. He winked. 'I'll kill him for you. Promise. He might be Death in human form to you but to me he's just another damn Yankee!'

Reluctantly Carver got back to his feet. He stared down at the man who did not look back at him. He knew that English would try his best to keep true to his word. Carver rubbed his dry mouth and then ran down into the tunnel.

Hope English heard the spurs getting fainter and fainter until there was no more sound. He closed one eye and looked down the long barrel. Every bone and sinew in the old soldier's body hurt and he wanted an end to his misery. Perhaps the man out there might provide him with the means to escape his pain, he thought.

Out in the mist Sunset knelt and tried to work out where his adversaries were. The mist which was giving him cover was also making it impossible for him to see anything ahead of him. He drew the Colt off his left hip, cocked its hammer and held it at arm's length. He stood up to his full height, then started to walk ahead.

'C'mon, *amigo*! Fire that carbine one more time so I can get a bead on you!' Sunset muttered to himself.

It took twenty strides before Johnny Sunset walked out of the mist and could see the hat on the head of the man who held the rifle. Sunlight danced along its long barrel. He knew that a few more steps and he would have the range with his .45. A few more steps.

'Shoot!' Sunset yelled out fiercely.

Squinting hard, English teased the trigger back. A circle of gunsmoke exploded around the Winchester barrel as it sent the lead bullet towards the defiant bounty hunter, Sunset felt the power of the bullet as it punched him off his feet. He landed on his back as the sound of the shot reached his ears. His Colt had flown out of his hand when he hit the sand. Sunset blinked and saw his weapon a few feet from his fingers.

There was no pain for a few seconds. Then it came with a vengeance and the bounty hunter curled up in agony. He rolled over and stared at the rifleman. The bullet had ripped the flesh off the top of his left shoulder but he refused to make any noise. As blood poured from the wound his shirt suddenly turned dark crimson.

'Damn it all!' the Sunset Kid cursed. 'I got that wrong!'

English pushed himself up and fired again.

The bullet kicked up the sand next to the bounty hunter's long frame. Sunset's fingers clawed the weapon up and shook sand from it. He could see the top half of the man and knew that the outlaw was within range.

He gritted his teeth against the pain and stared at his sleeve. It was soaked in blood. His hand was shaking as he lay on his side and tried to aim.

Sunset heard the sound of the rifle being readied again. He closed one eye and tried to focus on his target. For the first time in his life he doubted his ability. He rubbed the sweat from his brow and swallowed.

To the surprise of the bounty hunter, English moved higher above the rocks.

The sun glinted on the long-barrelled weapon as it was brought back to the outlaw's shoulder.

Johnny Sunset ignored his own pain and leapt to his feet again with the gun in his outstretched left hand. He saw the plume of smoke from the Winchester, then fired his own gun. He dropped down as the heat of the rifle bullet tore his Stetson off his head.

He had seen the outlaw knocked backwards. The rifle had flown into the air as English had disappeared behind the rocks.

'Got ya!' Sunset spat. 'Got ya dead centre!'

The bounty hunter rose to his feet once again and replaced the spent cartridge with a fresh bullet from his belt. His eyes never deviated from the rocks ahead until he was convinced that there were no other outlaws lying in wait for him.

Sunset dropped the Colt into its holster and then whistled.

He heard the stallion returning with

the packhorse in tow but still did not take his eyes off the outcrop of rocks. As the black horse reached his side he mounted and tapped his spurs.

The horse responded and galloped towards the rocks. Sunset touched the torn flesh of his shoulder as the stallion moved closer and closer to where he had last seen Hope English. He raised his fingers in front of his face and saw the blood on their tips.

He spurred harder.

As the stallion circled the rocks Sunset saw the outlaw lying on the sand in a pool of blood. Then he felt the ground begin to shake violently. For a moment he did not know what was happening. Then it all became crystal clear.

Moss Carver had done exactly as English had advised and blown up the tunnel entrance. The explosion sent smoke and debris showering into the hot morning air. The impact hit the rider off his horse and sent both horses crashing into the sand.

A stunned Sunset staggered to his feet and wiped the dust off his face just in time to see the gun in Hope English's right hand. The wounded outlaw had a bullet hole in him but was somehow still alive.

'Who are you, stranger?' the outlaw asked as he kept the gun trained on the tall man.

'The name's Sunset. Johnny Sunset.'

English gave a slow nod. 'I heard of you! Stinking bounty hunter, ain't you?'

'Yep.' Sunset nodded and helped his horse up off the sand. 'And you must be one of them bank robbers who took all of the money out of Silver City.'

'I'm one of them OK.' English could not get up from the sand. He just lay where he had landed and kept his six-shooter trained on the man who seemed to be more concerned with his horses than the thought of being killed at any moment. 'The name's English.'

Sunset looked at the man, 'Hope English? I seen your poster a while back. You got a two hundred dollar bounty on your head.'

English forced a smile. 'You know your trade, boy!'

'You gonna shoot me?'

'Yep!' English answered. 'I'm almost dead myself and a little company might be nice. Can't meet Satan on my lonesome.'

Sunset looked to the rubble which had only minutes earlier been the tunnel that led to the underground river. He then looked back at the dying outlaw.

'I don't understand why your cohorts done that. Why seal themselves into a trap like that?'

A faint smile crossed English's face. 'They ain't trapped, Sunset! They're on their way alongside a river down there!'

'On their way? Where to?'

'They'll come up in the middle of Deadman's Draw, Kid.' The outlaw told him. 'From there they can head down into Mexico. You'll have to ride into Deadman's Draw if'n you want to catch them! You can't follow them no more.

Your hunt is over.'

'I can try to follow.' Sunset rested the palm of his hand on the grip of the Colt and stared at the dying outlaw. 'Drop that gun or I'll have to draw.'

'Good!' English cocked the pistol.

Faster than the blink of an eye, Sunset drew and fanned his hammer. His Colt fired straight and true. English buckled and dropped his gun. The bounty hunter walked to the outlaw and looked down at him.

Defiantly, English was smiling.

'Thanks, Kid!' English said before his eyes rolled heavenward. 'I was praying you were good enough to finish me off!'

After watching the outlaw at his feet finally die, Johnny Sunset holstered his gun, turned and looked at his horses. He walked to them, stepped into his stirrup and swung his leg over the stallion's saddle.

He gathered up his reins and looked into the shimmering haze between himself and the infamous Deadman's Draw. Sunset tapped his spurs and reluctantly began to head towards the canyon flanked by two gigantic boulders of sand-coloured rock.

The sight ahead made him forget the cruel wound he now carried with him.

A coward would have quit.

Johnny Sunset spurred on.

13

There was no time for remorse. Men cut from the cloth that had created Moss Carver and his three followers never looked back unless there was someone chasing them. Since they had blown up the tunnel and made it impossible for anyone to follow them down into the long underground passageway into the depths of Deadman's Draw they had not even given Hope English a second thought. If he had survived it would be up to him to find them south of the border. If he had fallen victim to the mysterious rider, then they would simply divide his share of their loot between them.

Carver inhaled the sweet cool air which rose from the fast flowing river beside his horse and stared coldly ahead. He and the others carried a torch each to light up their way along the seemingly endless trail. He knew its twists and turns better than any of his cohorts, for unlike them he had remained sober each time they had ridden this route.

'How much further?' Fargo asked.

'Ain't far!' Carver replied as his boots continued to tap their spurs into the flesh of his horse.

Shale Davis guided his mount alongside Carver. He had a burning question that he had to ask. 'What in tarnation happened up there, Moss?'

'I had me a feeling we was being trailed!' Carver said. 'Me and Hope went up there and took us a look! I was right! Some varmint was following our trail!'

Davis gave a slow nod. 'I figured that but how come Hope stayed up there on his lonesome to kill the critter?'

'That's the way he wanted it, boy!' Carver spat. 'He ain't bin feeling good of late and I reckon he wanted to go out with his boots on!'

Davis looked at the hardened face

which refused to look back at him. 'Yeah, Hope was sure getting old! Too old to be of any use any more! Reckon his share of the money will add up to a tidy sum for us!'

Carver did not speak. His fist clenched and then smashed out and caught the younger outlaw across the jaw. Davis rocked on his saddle and dropped his torch. Blood ran down from his mouth as his blurred eyes tried to focus on Carver.

'W . . . what you do that for?'

Carver reined in. 'Pick up that torch!'

Davis could see the right hand of the angry horseman beside him curl around his holstered gun grip. See the index finger wrap itself around the trigger. He fearfully dismounted and staggered to where his torch lay on the ground. He picked it up and then began to walk back to his mount.

Fargo and Muller could also see Carver's hand on his gun. They knew that meant trouble. Neither of them spoke as they watched Davis haul himself back atop his horse and steady himself.

'You through bad-mouthing Hope, Shale?' Carver growled.

'Yep! I'm through!' Davis nervously nodded.

'Good!' Carver spat and glanced at the stunned rider. 'That means I don't have to kill you! Not right now, anyways!'

Davis felt his heart pounding inside his shirt. Carver jabbed his spurs into his horse and started again along the narrow trail beside the river. Fargo and Muller passed the dazed Davis as they trailed the man who could kill better than most when the urge took him. They knew how close the younger Davis had come to finding that out the hard way.

Like a whipped hound, Davis silently trailed them.

* * *

The sun was blazing like an inferno above them yet neither Skeet nor Will

Bower had the brains they had been born with. They continued to ride deeper and deeper into the land where death reigned supreme. Unlike the man they trailed they had not thought of buying a packhorse or stocking up with a supply of precious water. They had simply called in on Olaf Krugar and purchased two extra canteens, filled them and then headed out on their exhausted mounts.

The hoof-tracks left by the man known as the Sunset Kid were deep and clear. They lured the two wanted men like a bear to a beehive. Neither had considered the dangers they were heading into for they had only one thought between them and that was to kill the man who had killed their brothers. Few outlaws were blessed with less common sense than the entire Bower clan. As they continued to spur their lathered-up mounts into the haze of sickening illusion that only a desert can muster, they gave no heed to what they had embarked upon.

To face a bounty hunter as infamous as Sunset was foolhardy enough but to ride unprepared towards Deadman's Draw was totally unforgivable.

Their mounts had begun to slow hours earlier. Even before the sun had risen into the cloudless blue sky it would have been obvious to anyone with half a brain that their mounts were spent, but their masters had neither noticed or cared.

The dunes of soft golden sand were spread out all around the pair of hapless horsemen as they stopped for the umpteenth time to take refreshment from their canteens. Only this time there was not very much water to be had in any of them.

Will Bower gave a pained expression and then looked across at his equally confused brother.

'You got any water left, Skeet?' Will asked. He shook his canteen before casting it over his shoulder.

Skeet swallowed the last of the warm liquid and then shook his canteen as if he might be able to magically create more inside the empty container.

'Nope! I'm out!'

Will rubbed his whiskered jaw and rested an elbow on his saddle horn. His eyes were staring around them at the vast expanse of sand which now reached every horizon.

'Reckon there's a well someplace around here?'

'Now that's a thought I've bin pondering.' Skeet tossed his empty canteen away with the same lack of imagination that his brother had displayed seconds earlier. Neither sibling had thought that if they did discover water they might just require a vessel to put it into. Something like canteens.

Far to their right they could see buzzards circling on high thermals but again the riders were incapable of reading the signs.

Will aimed a finger at the hoof-tracks in the sand. 'Sunset must know where to find water, Skeet. Why else would he ride this way?'

Skeet nodded in agreement. 'Damn right. Sunset ain't loco. I figure he'll lead us straight to a lake or something kin to a lake.'

'I'm sure thirsty though.'

'Me too!'

Both riders were about to jab their spurs into their horses when Skeet's animal staggered forward and toppled on to its knees. The outlaw went straight over the neck and head of the horse and landed on his face in the hot burning sand.

Will threw a leg over the neck of his own mount and slid down to the sand.

'Hey! This nag of yours looks kinda worn out!'

Skeet Bower turned and spat sand. He looked at the creature which he had not considered worthy of watering since they had left Silver City. He rubbed his head and then got back to his feet.

'Reckon you might be right!'

'What we gonna do if'n our nags

both fold up and die, Skeet? I don't hanker on being out here in this sand heap without a nag under my rump! It's kinda hot!'

The older Bower rubbed his neck and looked straight up at the blue sky.

'What did Ma always tell us, Will?'

'The Lord will provide!' Will Bower said quickly.

'Exactly!' Skeet Bower leaned over and dragged his long Winchester from its scabbard beneath the horse's saddle. 'The Lord will provide and I reckon he's providing right now!'

The younger brother scratched his head. 'You had too much sun or something, Skeet?'

Skeet Bower gave a wry smile, then pointed to his left. Will raised a hand and shielded his eyes against the sun. For a few moments he could not see anything. Then he saw them. Five near-naked riders were fringing a dune about a half-mile from where the two men stood.

'Damn it all!' Will gasped. 'Injuns!'

'Injuns with horses and what looks like waterbags.' Skeet cranked his rifle, looked into its magazine and started counting. 'I got me about ten bullets in this thing. How many rounds you got in your rifle?'

Will staggered across the sand. He pulled his own rifle from under his saddle and looked at it. 'I think I got me about the same. Why?'

'Think about it. If we wait until they gets a tad closer we can shoot most of them and then steal their best mounts and water.'

Will Bower cranked his rifle. 'What if they got rifles?'

'Injuns don't use rifles!' Skeet sighed. 'They use bows and arrows. Damn! You sure are dumb.'

'I'm thirsty,' Will growled loudly. 'OK?'

'OK!' Skeet shrugged. 'C'mon!'

Both men left their horses and started to move behind the cover of a dune. They slowly climbed up the sifting sand until they reached the top.

Both men lay down and aimed.
  'Turkey shoot!' Skeet smiled.
  'Candy from babies!'
  They were both wrong.

14

There was a hushed silence across the desert. Whether the Apache hunting party had seen the outlaws Skeet and Will Bower no one would never know. They certainly did not appear to want to make contact with either man. They had steered their mounts away from the place where the wanted men and their horses had stopped and were clearly headed in a different direction. A direction designed to avoid any possibility of an encounter occurring.

But to men like the Bowers it meant nothing that others might be attempting to avoid trouble. They had never respected anyone and killed whenever they wanted to.

Both men aimed their rifles at the line of five Apache horsemen as they peacefully steered their ponies across the top of a dune 200 yards away.

Without any warning the outlaws began to fire. Their bullets raced through the hot air and cut into their targets mercilessly. They laughed triumphantly as two of the braves were hit by their lead and fell from their mounts before rolling down the dune. Two lines of red marked the golden sand.

Then their laughter ceased.

Neither of the Bower's had encountered Apaches before or tasted their wrath. Their entire knowledge of the small sturdy warriors was built on hearsay. They were to learn the truth the hard way. The three remaining braves swiftly dropped from their ponies and began to charge at their attackers. To the complete horror of the Bower brothers, the Indians did have rifles.

Rifles they knew how to use.

Deafening, lethal lead came back in reply as the three sun-baked men managed not only to run but aim and fire in a fluid action that neither of the outlaws had ever imagined possible.

The war cries which came from the charging braves echoed around the desolation and filled both outlaws with terror.

Bullets tore up the sand all around them.

Will Bowers slid down as one of the shots tore not only his Stetson from his head but part of his scalp. The chunk of bleeding flesh hung over his face.

Skeet tried to find a target but the volley of bullets forced him to keep his head down. He glanced at his sibling, then stared in stunned shock when he saw the brutal wound across the top of Will's head.

'You OK?'

'No I damn well ain't! You said they only had bows and arrows!' Will screamed as he felt the blood pouring down from his cranium over his dust-caked face.

Skeet blinked hard as the sound of the Indians got louder.

'Well, that's what folks say.'

'C'mon! We gotta kill the whole bunch of them or they'll do for us!' Will gritted his yellow teeth and swung round on the sand. He began to crawl back up to where the sand was being churned up by a ceaseless barrage of bullets.

Skeet followed his brother to the top of the dune. Both outlaws primed their rifles and began to unleash their own lead in blind dread. They both knew that they had opened a can of worms which neither of them had imagined.

Both outlaws fired their rifles time after time in an attempt to fend off the men they knew would make them pay the ultimate price for killing two of the hunting party. Bullets tore back as the entire dune became drowned in choking gunsmoke.

Skeet felt himself knocked back as a bullet cut into him but he did not stop firing. When his rifle was empty he simply discarded it; then he dragged both his guns from their holsters and began using them.

The air tasted like poison.

It was virtually impossible to see the

men who still charged at them. Bullets tore through the air in both directions without a second's pause.

Then one of the howling braves suddenly came hurtling out of the gunsmoke and hit Will off his feet. Rifles and guns flew into the air. They both tumbled down the dune and did not stop until they were next to the outlaws' horses.

A knife-blade flashed in the sunlight.

Will Bower had never had to fight for his life before. Never had to wrestle a man to the death, but that was what he found himself doing as the blade's lethal edge slashed into his arms and legs as the two men grappled in furious battle. A moccasin came up and pushed the outlaw backward. Will staggered and then clenched both fists. This time he managed to catch the jaw of the brave. A loud sound of cracking bone filled the air. The punch knocked the Apache down but then the knife lashed out again and ripped the outlaw's shirt apart.

Blood splashed across the sand as the two men locked together again in combat. This time the stronger Indian managed to force his opponent down. Although Will Bower held the wrists of the Indian firmly he could see the knife blade getting closer and closer to his throat.

Above them Skeet kept firing until there were no more shots coming at him. His screwed-up eyes saw the dead braves less than twenty feet from where he stood.

The outlaw swung round and looked down at his brother as he fought the Indian feverishly below. The outlaw took a step, then he felt the pain in his leg rip through his entire being.

Skeet fell and began to slide down the dune towards the two fighting men. He aimed both his six-shooters and squeezed their triggers at the same time.

His two bullets hit the last of the Apaches high in his gleaming back. The dark-skinned warrior arched and then went limp as he slumped off Will and fell into the sand.

Will Bower raised his blood-soaked head off the sand and looked wearily at his brother. They were both drenched in their own gore.

'We get them all?'

Skeet nodded. 'Yep!'

'Reckon we better try and catch their horses!' Will managed to get to his feet. He rubbed the blood from his face as the scalp wound continued to pump the crimson evidence of his brutal battle over his clothing.

Skeet looked at his leg. 'I got me a hole right through my leg, Will! You better go catch them on your lonesome.'

The younger of the brothers marched to Skeet and held out a hand. 'Git on your damn feet, Skeet. I ain't catching them nags alone. You savvy?'

Skeet allowed his angry brother to haul him up. 'But my leg hurts darn bad, Will!'

'Then limp!' Will shouted.

15

The echoes of the brief but bloody battle rang out all around the bounty hunter. It mocked his senses into trying to work out where it had originated. Johnny Sunset stood in his stirrups and vainly stared out into the heat haze to his left. That seemed to be the place where he had first heard the cracking of Winchesters but he knew the desert played tricks on the weary — and he was weary. He was also wounded. The blood had already dried under the incessant rays of the sun but it still stung like fury. A thousand hornets could not have matched the pain which nagged at the tall rider. Fine grains of sand blown across the expanse of desert stuck to the wound and burned.

The powerful stallion beneath him waited as its master tried to fathom who had been shooting so vigorously.

He had thought that he had heard Indian war cries but now doubted his own memory.

Slowly the horseman lowered himself back down on to his saddle and gathered up the reins to the packhorse behind his black mount. He looped the long leathers around his saddle horn and licked his cracked lips. The day was less than thirty minutes old but it felt as though he had been here for hours.

Again the questions burned into his mind.

Sunset knew that Carver and what remained of his gang were somewhere below the sun-baked sand, making good their escape. The only member of the bank robbers to remain on the blistering surface of the desert now was attracting buzzards and flies.

So who was it that had been firing rifles and six-shooters behind him?

The lean rider rubbed the sweat from his dust-caked features and brooded over the unanswerable question. His mind raced as he tapped his spurs and started the stallion again on the almost suicidal journey into the jaws of Deadman's Draw.

The mountainous golden rockfaces to either side loomed like monsters from some ancient fable but Sunset did not seem to notice. His thoughts were on the rifle fire which still rang out off the towering sides of the infamous canyon.

Without even noticing, the bounty hunter had entered the place from which, it was reputed, no man ever escaped. He allowed his sturdy horse to find its own pace and kept looking backward to where he imagined the shooting had occurred.

Was he being followed?

If so, by whom?

And if he were being trailed, who on earth were his followers fighting?

Sweat flowed like rain from every pore in his body as the stallion proceeded onward. His shirt and pants were soaked until they were like another layer of flesh clinging to his skin. Yet even the sores which came from the drying salt inside his trail gear did not trouble him.

His mind was elsewhere, in a place where questions had no answers that made any sense.

Doubts that he was even heading in the right direction began to haunt the rider as he travelled mile after endless mile deeper into the deadly canyon.

How did he know that Carver and his boys were heading this way at all?

Sunset had only the word of a dying outlaw that Carver was headed into the canyon at all. Was it possible that there could be an underground river below such arid terrain? Would Hope English have wasted his last breath lying?

Sunset looked away from what lay behind them and concentrated on the scenery ahead. He felt his heart quicken as the true menace of Deadman's Draw overwhelmed him. He glanced to both sides at the soaring sand coloured rocks. They looked as though every ounce of moisture had been sucked from them since Satan had created them.

Wisps of dust blew off them as the strange continuous breeze channelled along the length of the canyon. Boulders on the sand to both sides of him indicated that the rocks were crumbling and could fall at any time.

Then he saw the bones.

White bones half-buried by drifting sand. They were scattered about everywhere.

Sunset swallowed hard and tried to estimate how long this trail between mountains of rock might take him. There was no way he could estimate anything within the long natural corridor of rock. What lay ahead was bathed in a heat haze which tormented the eyes and bewildered the mind. He glanced over his wounded shoulder at the packhorse in a vain attempt to satisfy himself that he had enough water to last. No matter how many times he looked at the damp waterbags Sunset failed.

He tapped his spurs and managed to get his mount to increase its pace. There was no reason to make the stallion move faster but the bounty hunter began to be fearful.

Fearful that this canyon would add him to its tally of victims whatever he did. Death dwelled in Deadman's Draw. It did not ride a black horse as Moss Carver had imagined but still had many ways of killing even those who were aware of its power. He reached down and plucked his canteen from the saddle horn, unscrewed its stopper and downed its last few precious drops of liquid. He knew that he would have to refill it soon from one of the bags on his pack-animal but did not want to slow his pace until there was no other option.

The heat was unceasing. It drained the rider. Sunset felt as though his brain were frying under his Stetson. Wisdom escaped from him like the sweat which flowed from every pore of his skin. There was no way of knowing what was either right or wrong in such a lethal place.

Was it smarter to ride fast to cut the journey time down or slow up and allow his animals to remain as fit as possible? He cursed silently before the thought of the men he hunted returned to his fevered mind.

Again he looked all about him.

What was he doing in a hellhole such as this?

Was he riding to his own death?

Sunset reined back. The gleaming black animal responded and slowed down. The packhorse snorted as though in thanks. The bounty hunter glanced down at his brand-new gun in its custom-made holster on his right hip. A wry knowing smile etched the young rider's features. So far he had not even tested the weapon but he knew that when he did it would do its job.

'Where are they?' Sunset asked the dry air.

There was no knowing whether he might ever catch up with his prey, for he had no idea where they would appear along the canyon.

Every stride of the stallion appeared to bring him no closer to anything but more sand. It was as though he were caught in a sweat-soaked nightmare. No matter how fast he might go, his magnificent horse's hoofs remained glued to the spot.

Sunset had heard the word 'suicidal' when he had said he was going to trail the outlaws into this hostile land known as Deadman's Draw.

Now it seemed to be more than just a word.

The bounty hunter glanced at the sun. It was still hours before it would reach its zenith. Hours before it would be directly overhead and even hotter than it was now.

The horseman whirled his reins over the stallion's head and kept his mount moving. He knew that he must already have travelled several miles into this sweltering cauldron but fretted over how much further there was to go.

When would he encounter the men he tracked?

Sunset forced himself up until he was standing in his stirrups once more. The fine grains of sand which blew along the canyon gnawed into his face but he ignored the pain and drove his animal on.

Now the doubts were gone. Now he could think of only one thing and that was getting his hands on the outlaws and dishing out his own brand of retribution.

'C'mon, boy!' Johnny Sunset yelled at the top of his voice to his thundering mount. 'We got us a lot of bounty to collect!'

16

Johnny Sunset had not suspected that Deadman's Draw held a far greater danger than either the canyon's deadly heat or the eventual encountering of the ruthless Carver gang as he balanced in his stirrups and galloped around a rocky bend. But it did hold one other peril no one could ever have imagined possible. The eyes of the expert horseman widened in total disbelief as he saw them twenty yards ahead. The sound of his horses' hoofs had echoed all along the canyon trail and alerted the line of Apache who knelt with their bows taut and arrows in readiness. Their number spanned the entire width of the canyon.

Sunset dragged on his reins and sat down on to his saddle. He could not believe the terrifying apparition which faced him: at least twenty braves with their arrows aimed straight at him.

The rider blinked hard as though the heat were playing tricks with his eyes. But this was no mirage. No trick of the light. No mere delusion.

This was real.

They were real.

All the legends about this unholy place were wrong. Somehow these men with sun-baked skin could and did live in Deadman's Draw. Perhaps it was one of the few places remaining where they could exist. A place into which not even the greediest of white men would willing venture.

Sweat ran down his chiselled features.

Sunset steadied his stallion and tried to think. His eyes darted from one face to the next until he had looked at them all in turn. Not one face showed any sign of emotion. Each was as though it were carved from stone.

'Howdy!' Sunset drawled.

There was no response.

Again his heart missed a beat. He

was in trouble. Real big trouble.

He wondered if it were possible to turn his black horse and flee before they let loose with their arrows. The bounty hunter knew that no man could ever achieve that feat and live. There was not a horse alive who could run as fast as an Apache arrow.

His heart pounded.

He knew that any movement towards his guns might provoke them into unleashing their arrows. He could not afford to lose any more blood in this desolate place.

Sighing, Johnny Sunset resigned himself to the fact that his destiny was now in the hands of the men who had their arrows trained upon him. Slowly he looped his reins around his saddle horn and raised his hands.

They showed no emotion.

'Damn it all!' Sunset cursed.

Then they slowly began to rise.

The bounty hunter licked his dry, cracked lips and glanced at his pack-horse and the water bags. He had tried

to outwit this infamous land. Now that
seemed to be totally pointless.

★   ★   ★

Ten miles north-west of Deadman's
Draw the Bower brothers had dispatched the hunting party without a
second thought. There was a lot of
blood on the otherwise golden sand.
The bodies of the five innocent
Apaches were strewn across the baking-
hot ground all around the two wounded
outlaws. The Bower brothers had
managed to catch three of the Indian
ponies and were drinking their fill of
their victims' water.

The sun was blazing down upon the
bodies as Skeet Bower threw his saddle
across the back of the nervous Indian
pony and tightened the cinch strap
beneath its belly. He then dragged the
rope from the head of the small animal
and exchanged it for his own bridle.
The animal tried to fight against his
new master but it was in vain. The elder

163

of the Bower brothers showed no mercy to the small pony. He soon mounted the creature and rammed his vicious spurs into its flesh.

The animal tried to escape from the pain but Skeet Bower held it firmly in check.

Will Bower had not bothered to use one of the dead Apaches' ponies but watered and grained his own mount until it was refreshed enough to be mounted again.

Will held his horse steady, then patted the full waterbag across his saddle cantle. He glanced at his brother and nodded firmly. Skeet returned the nod. They were both covered in their own dried blood as well as the rotting gore of their dead foes, but sitting atop rested mounts neither outlaw thought about his own injuries.

Now all they could think of was the man they had trailed to this desolate place. Johnny Sunset's tracks were still clearly evident in the sand which led towards the distant mass of golden rocks.

Skeet had salvaged all the waterbags from the three ponies he and his brother had managed to catch. Both riders gave a silent nod and rammed their spurs into the flanks of their mounts. The horses thundered into action and started to plough through the sand in pursuit of their prey.

Unlike the man they were hunting, the brothers did not have the intelligence to fear either the desert or any of its many ways of destroying living creatures.

As they rode on through the churned-up sand in chase of the bounty hunter who had already proved his deadly ability against their dead siblings, neither of them had any idea of what they were racing blindly towards.

The outlaws wanted revenge and there was only one certain way of getting it. They had to kill the man who had left their brothers back at San Carlos with his lead in them.

They spurred hard.

The horses responded as all fearful

animals do when trying to outrun the spurs of their ruthless masters. They raced across the sand as the vicious sharp spurs kicked back into them over and over again.

Neither outlaw knew that they were racing to a place where only death was a certainty. Whose death might the Grim Reaper satisfy himself with?

As the sun continued to rise high into the cloudless blue heavens their shadows grew shorter. The heat they had already endured was nothing compared to the temperature the sun would eventually torment them with at noon.

Then there would be no shadows.

Nowhere to hide.

17

They said nothing but moved like phantoms towards the horseman with their arrows still aimed straight at him. Sunset realized that any one of the archers could kill him at any time, but he was strangely unafraid. He knew that if an arrow left its bow he would probably not know anything about it. It would be an instant death with no lingering torment such as came from being bitten by a poisonous sidewinder. These were men who were probably more deadly with their bows than he was with his Colt.

They surrounded him.

There was no possibility of escape.

Sunset felt the sweat tracing down his spine beneath his already sodden shirt. His eyes moved from one of their faces to the next. Again their unblinking hooded eyes set in emotionless faces showed no sign of animation. Frozen features which could have made even the best riverboat gambler realize what the term 'poker face' actually meant gazed at him.

The horseman wondered why they had not already killed him. They had had plenty of opportunity to do so. He watched as they moved around him. Their silent bare feet did not seem to feel the heat of the sand as they moved all around his two horses. Sunset turned his head and saw another Apache warrior close to the jagged canyon wall to his right. Unlike those who encircled him, this one wore a feathered head-dress and did not approach.

Sunset concentrated on this Apache who was either a medicine man or a chief. Either way, he seemed to look more important than those who had him covered.

The bounty hunter pulled his right boot from its stirrup and then slowly raised his leg until it cleared the neck of his motionless stallion.

Cautiously Sunset slid from his saddle and landed between his two horses. For a moment he just remained where he had landed and waited for his captors to strike.

Again they did nothing except watch.

Sunset had only once encountered Apaches before and that had been more than five years earlier. It had taught him that it was best not to start an unprovoked fight with them. Few men survived such battles.

The bounty hunter towered over the bowmen. Not one of them stood more than five feet in height yet every sinew of their bodies could be seen.

Then the obvious dawned on Sunset.

They were starving. Either that or damn hungry.

Protruding ribs and swollen bellies meant only one thing and that was malnutrition. The bounty hunter glanced across at the man in the head-dress and nodded at him.

There was no reaction.

Taking his life in his hands, Sunset turned and walked to his saddle-bags. He opened one of the satchels. He pulled out the bags of aromatic dried jerky and hardtack biscuits which he had brought with him and walked through the bowmen towards the Apache who remained beside the sand coloured canyon wall.

With every stride Sunset took as he walked towards the tribal leader, the bowmen trailed him with their deadly flint arrowheads still aimed at him.

When Sunset reached the warrior in the headdress he stopped and held the food out to the silent warrior.

'It ain't much, but it's all I got! Do you want it?' Sunset asked.

The man in the feathered head-dress raised both his hands and signalled to two of his men. They lowered their bows, rushed in and took the bags from the bounty hunter.

Again nothing was said by any of them.

Johnny Sunset rubbed the grime

from his face and glanced around at the other warriors. They had now all lowered their lethal bows and removed the arrows from the weapons' strings.

The Apache elder touched his chest and made a waving gesture with his hand. The bounty hunter nodded and returned to his mount. They watched as the tall, lean man stepped into his stirrup and pulled himself up on to the black stallion before he gathered the reins of his packhorse.

Sunset tapped his spurs.

They parted and allowed the horseman to continue on his way along the trail which felt as though it had no end. The stallion had barely gone 200 yards when Sunset looked over his wounded shoulder into the swirling mist to the spot where he had imagined his life would end.

To his utter surprise not one of the Indians was there any longer. Just the heat haze which mocked his eyes. He eased back on his reins and stopped the magnificent horse in its tracks. It seemed that Deadman's Draw held even more secrets.

Then he heard the rifle fire.

Johnny Sunset looked back along the trail he had yet to travel and saw the darkened images of men as they appeared to emerge from the ground itself. One man held a smoking rifle in his hands and continued to fire at the horseman. Chunks of stone were torn from the canyon wall beside him. Debris and dust showered over the bounty hunter as his horse reared up and kicked out in fury.

Then Sunset heard the pitiful sound of his packhorse as one of the deadly outlaws bullets hit it. The animal staggered, then fell beside the skittish stallion.

The smell of fresh blood filled the nostrils of both horse and rider.

Sunset jumped from his mount and dropped behind the wounded pack-horse. He drew his .45 and cocked its hammer just as a rifle shot hit one of his waterbags. A fountain of the precious liquid squirted up into dry canyon air.

The bounty hunter got up on to one knee and started to return fire into the sickening vapour which shielded his attackers from a sure shot.

He had wasted five bullets before he managed to hit one of the Carver gang. The wailing of a man who had taken a lead ball echoed all around the towering sides of the canyon walls. Sunset dropped back down and shook the casings from his smoking gun before reloading with bullets from his belt.

Just as he pushed the last of the bullets into the gun's hot cylinder he heard the sound of hoofs thundering away. The young bounty hunter leapt to his feet and grabbed at the reins to the black stallion.

'Easy, horse!' he shouted.

The skittish animal continued to rear up. Sunset grabbed hold of his saddle horn as his mount started to run. He threw himself atop the galloping horse and rode into the mist.

'C'mon, boy!' Sunset urged. 'There ain't a horse alive you can't catch!'

The wide-eyed thoroughbred knew what its master wanted and increased its pace with every stride. Johnny Sunset leaned into the black mane and hung on.

18

The bullet had found its mark even though the bounty hunter had not even seen his target during the explosion of lead which had erupted from Carver and his gang's guns. Blood pumped from the viscid hole in Ben Fargo's chest as the outlaw hung over the neck of his horse and vainly attempted to keep up with Muller, Davis and Carver as they careered along the baking-hot canyon. Fargo had been the last of the four outlaws to lead his mount out of the underground cavern and that simple fact had been why Sunset's sixth bullet had found him.

The wounded outlaw's eyes began to dim as life evaporated from him faster than water disappeared on the desert floor. Somehow he had managed to mount his horse after the bullet had knocked him backwards into the canyon wall but it had been a futile gesture for no man's heart was strong enough to take a bullet.

The refreshed horse beneath him was charging after the three other outlaws' mounts but the pounding of its muscular legs just shook even more blood from the mortally wounded rider.

Fargo had called out to them when the bounty hunter's shot had hit him but they had ignored his calls for help. Like most of their breed they looked after themselves and gave little heed to anyone else. Fargo's eyes gazed through the choking dust of his fellow outlaws' mounts. They were now a score of yards ahead of him and getting further away with every passing beat of his slowing heart.

Then the sound behind him filled Fargo's ears. He could hear the bounty hunter getting closer and closer. Barely able to balance on the galloping horse Fargo somehow managed to turn and look back through his own dust at the black stallion and its grim-faced rider thundering after him.

Yet even though he was mortally wounded the outlaw instincts wanted nothing more than to fend off anyone who had the mettle to challenge him. His blood-soaked left hand reached down and dragged his Winchester from its scabbard but the hefty weapon slipped from his grip as soon as it cleared the long leather sheath.

In desperation he drew one of his six-shooters from its holster and cocked its hammer. He tilted his maimed body, aimed and squeezed the trigger. The sheer power of the weapon in his hand was too much for the weakened outlaw. He felt himself flying from the saddle.

Fargo hit the sand-coloured rocks but he did not feel anything. Death had spared him that final agony. He slid to the sand like a broken doll.

Johnny Sunset charged past the dead man lying against the canyon wall and spurred. He soon overtook the riderless horse and saw the moneybags tied securely to its saddle. He whipped the shoulders of his stallion with the ends of his long leathers and pressed on after the three remaining men whose dust he was eating.

The bounty hunter knew that he was catching up with the outlaws because he could now see them clearly. The foggy haze of baking-hot air could no longer veil them in its sickening cloak of mystery.

But Sunset knew that if he could see them it followed that they could also see him. He leaned over the neck of his potent charger and allowed the animal its head. The stallion responded with an even greater turn of speed.

A long winding corner saw the canyon walls grow further apart as the almost sheer walls towered higher than anywhere else within the boundaries of the place known as Deadman's Draw.

Then he saw the glinting of handguns in the outlaws' hands as they tried to train their weaponry on their pursuer. Sunset steered his mount in a zigzag fashion as it closed down on his prey.

A shot rang out.

Then a handful more.

Hot lead whizzed down the canyon from their guns. But each bullet went either high or wide of its mark.

'C'mon!' Sunset urged his powerful mount. 'We got these critters beat, boy!'

The black stallion began to find a pace which few other horses could ever have equalled and none manage to better. It raced through the gunsmoke as more bullets were fired at the bounty hunter.

Unlike Sunset the three outlaws were all right-handed. They each had turned to their right and stretched in order to fire their guns. Being an expert rider, Sunset instinctively steered his horse to the opposite side of the canyon, knowing that the riders would have to switch gun hands to get a bullet even close to him. As the Carver gang had more than enough work to do just keeping their horses at full speed, Sunset doubted any of them would dare try.

It seemed impossible but the Sunset Kid began to think that it was getting even hotter the further along the deadly trail he rode. He screwed up his eyes and looked at the horses ahead of him and their shadows. Shadows which were now directly beneath the galloping animals.

It was midday.

Noon and the sun was at its highest. The stallion began to close in on Shale Davis and his sweat-sodden mount. Davis was ten yards behind Sol Muller who in turn was twice that distance behind Moss Carver. Davis was losing ground to them both and knew it. Frantically he glanced over his shoulder and saw the fearsome rider behind him.

It was a determined Sunset who lowered his right gloved hand and gripped his saddle horn. He steadied himself and allowed the black mount to do what it did best. The powerful stallion charged on at breakneck pace beneath him as Sunset drew his Colt with his left hand and cocked its hammer.

He held his outstretched arm over the neck of his stallion and aimed at the outlaw. Each stride of the black horse ate up the distance between them until both animals were almost level and separated by a dozen or so feet.

As the pair of horses raced neck and neck, Davis swung around with his smoking Colt in his hand and blasted a shot at the bounty hunter. Sunset ducked as the small lead ball barely missed him.

Sunset steadied his Colt and then squeezed its trigger.

His aim was true.

He watched his bullet hit Shale Davis in the middle of his temple. The outlaw shook as his skull shattered beneath his Stetson.

Davis's lifeless body was lifted off his saddle and appeared to float for a few seconds before falling and then smashing into the ground. Again Sunset noted the moneybags tied to the horse's saddle. He saw the mount suddenly slow when it realized it no longer had a rider astride its broad back. The bounty hunter leaned over the neck of his mount and stood in his stirrups. Now with the weight on his horse's shoulders he knew the animal would find even more speed.

This was now a race. A race that only one of the horses had been bred to win.

Within a minute Sunset was closing in on Sol Muller. But unlike Davis, Muller had no desire to have his head blown off his shoulders. And, what was more, Muller was a far better horseman than his dead cohort.

The outlaw grabbed his saddle horn with his left hand, swung his left leg over the saddle cantle and then crouched down along the right side of his mount as it continued to gallop after Carver. Muller steered his mount close to the jagged canyon rockface knowing that there was now no target for the bounty hunter to aim at.

Johnny Sunset could barely see the

182

rider as he drew level with the running horse. The only thing visible was the gloved hand which gripped the saddle horn. Some might have tried to shoot the outlaw's hand but not Sunset. There was too much chance of hitting the mount and Sunset had never liked anyone who harmed horseflesh.

There had to be another way.

The bounty hunter eased his reins back, gritted his teeth and kept his own mount level with Muller's horse. He had seen trick-riding many times in his life and knew that many of the plains Indians used this particular trick to make onlookers believe a horse had no rider.

As both horses charged along the canyon Sunset pulled his gun hammer back again until it fully locked. He glanced up and could see that the other outlaw was now getting away as he remained alongside Muller's mount.

The stallion was champing on its bit and Sunset had to make a decision. He relaxed his grip on his reins and his mount began to leave Muller's horse in its wake. But Sunset knew that the outlaw was only waiting for the opportunity to put lead into his back. As the stallion put ten yards between itself and Muller's lathered-up horse the bounty hunter showed his own ability for trick riding.

He pulled his left boot from its stirrup and swung around until he was virtually facing backwards. Just like Muller, Sunset was balancing his entire weight on one stirrup. He screwed up his eyes and saw the outlaw raise his gun and shoot.

The hot lead went high and Sunset instantly returned fire. Even the dust could not hide the stunned expression on Muller's face as the bounty hunter's bullet hit him in his chest.

Muller fell from the horse and rolled over a dozen times before coming to a bloody rest in the hot, golden sand.

Johnny Sunset threw his leg over his mount's back and rammed his boot into the stirrup once again. He dropped the smoking .45 back into his holster, then gathered up his reins in his hands. He spurred and started on after the last of the men he hunted.

But the delay had cost Johnny Sunset time and distance.

Moss Carver had managed to put hundreds of yards between himself and the rider on his trail. Now the swirling heat haze had come back to shield the outlaw.

Relentlessly, Sunset pressed on and galloped after the last of the wanted men. His faithful horse obeyed every command of its master and raced into the fog which separated both horsemen.

As the steaming air parted for a few brief seconds ahead of the bounty hunter, Sunset felt his horse shy. The honed instincts of the rider realized that something was wrong. Seriously wrong.

Then he saw it.

A stick of lethal dynamite lay in the middle of the expanse of sand with a fuse wire smouldering and sparking from its core.

Johnny Sunset hauled back on his reins just as the dynamite erupted into devastating fury.

The explosion was ferocious. It sent burning sand out in all directions as its shock waves rocked the fragile rocks of the canyon walls. The stallion was stopped in its tracks and crashed into the ground.

The power of the blast hit the rider even harder. Sunset rolled over a dozen or more times before his bleeding body stopped. No mule could have kicked harder. The stunned hunter of men managed to force his face out of the sand when he heard another sound. A rumbling which shook the very heart of Deadman's Draw from top to bottom.

Boulders began to fall from the dry canyon walls. A few at first and then more and more.

Soon it was raining rocks of every shape and size. Choking dust soon replaced the heat haze as the avalanche of rocks bounced all around him.

Sunset crawled across the sand

towards his horse as boulders smashed into the sand all around him. Then he saw the shape of a man a hundred yards ahead. Even though he was stunned and dazed the bounty hunter recognized the outlaw. His image was branded into his memory like all the others he had seen on wanted posters.

'Carver!' he spat.

No sooner had he recognized the outlaw when the smoke from the deep crater swirled between the adversaries.

Johnny Sunset used the smoking crater in the centre of the wide canyon floor to his advantage. He kept low and quickly crawled towards his fallen mount. He had already seen the unmistakable Moss Carver up the trail, watching the fruits of his labour tear the heart out of the desert canyon. Now Sunset had to think of a way of killing him.

But men like Carver never died easy.

They would fight to their last drop of blood and then some.

With rocks still cascading all around

him the lean Sunset now knew that the outlaw was quite capable of doing anything. His years of training in the war had taught him more than most men would ever learn about killing. Nothing was sacred to men like Carver.

Sunset reached the side of his bleeding horse and ran his hands over the bleeding animal to check whether it had any broken bones. It seemed that, like himself, the creature was simply stunned and had suffered countless cuts from the brutal blast.

Apart from that, Sunset knew it could still carry him out of this unholy place, if the outlaw did not shoot it first.

The black stallion went to rise when Sunset placed a hand upon its neck and held it down. The animal was bleeding but the bounty hunter knew that should it get back to its feet the outlaw would surely place a rifle bullet into it.

Carver was no fool, he knew that even the best bounty hunter in the West was a dead man without a horse under his backside in this merciless terrain.

'Easy, boy!' Sunset said into the stallion's ear as even more boulders fell and rolled across the blackened sand around them. 'We gotta think this through!'

But the horse was strong and wanted to rise. Sunset knew that there was a limit to how long he could keep the animal on the sand.

'Stay still and that varmint will think he's done for you!' Sunset told the horse. His eyes darted all around the area as though searching for a clue to what he might do to escape this unexpected snag in his otherwise perfect plan.

The sides of the canyon looked as though they were ready to collapse completely at any given moment. In such a confined place the single stick of dynamite had weakened the already dry rocks severely.

Then as the smoke drifted away from the crater he saw that Carver was holding a rifle in his hands. The long barrel glinted like precious metal as the sunlight filled every inch of Deadman's Draw.

'Damn it all!' Sunset cursed at the sight of the Winchester in the outlaw's grasp. 'He's got his carbine out and you're lying on my rifle, boy! That critter can riddle us both with lead and my .45 ain't gonna make half the range!'

The stallion snorted as its master lay across its neck.

'What's he gonna do?' Sunset asked the subdued animal. 'He's got us beat if'n we stay at this distance!'

Then Johnny Sunset saw Carver react to shifting boulders above his own head. He was forced to backstep as rocks fell close to where he stood. At the same moment Sunset also caught sight of the outlaw's horse laden down with well-stuffed moneybags. Sunset knew that the outlaw's attention had been temporarily drawn away from him and his horse and that offered him an opportunity he could not afford to waste. The bounty hunter quickly dragged his rope from the saddle horn and swiftly looped it around the legs of the stallion until the creature was hogtied.

He tightened it and tossed the slack aside. Now he knew the horse would be unable to stand. That might just prevent it becoming Carver's next chosen target, Sunset thought.

The bounty hunter looked down at the pristine gun on his right hip. The converted double-barrelled scattergun had yet to be tested and it was still of no use in this situation. The deadly weapon had less than half the range of his Colt. But he was determined that he would get to use the gun before he himself was killed.

Sunset dropped on to his belly.

Using the crater smoke as cover, he started to crawl away from the horse. He moved like a sidewinder across the burning hot sand towards the nearest of the canyon walls. Boulders still fell but now the bounty hunter felt it was time to risk getting closer to his prey.

It was better to die trying than just waiting to be picked off.

Smoke drifted all around the area. It moved as though it were alive. The constant breeze which ran the entire length of the canyon gave no relief to the blistering heat which filled the confines of this hellish place, but it did mask the man who lay low and continued to crawl ever closer to Carver.

When Sunset reached the canyon wall he stood and reached his full height. Rocks still rained down but now they were smaller and less fearsome.

He pressed his back against the jagged rockface. Pain from innumerable cuts tormented his entire body but Sunset kept on edging along towards the place where he had last seen Carver.

Without pausing for a single moment, his left hand pulled the Colt from its holster and started to reload. He plucked the spent casings from the smoking gun and replaced them with fresh bullets from his gunbelt.

Sunset knew that every step brought Carver closer to being in range of his trusty six-shooter. If he got close enough he might even draw the scattergun. Each sideways step brought the risk that the deadly outlaw would spot him. If that happened before he was in range, Carver's Winchester would make short work of him.

This was no ordinary outlaw he was closing in upon. Sunset knew that men who had endured war were different from most wanted outlaws with hefty rewards on their heads. They had learned to survive the impossible and never quit.

Suddenly the sound of the rifle's mechanism being readied stopped the tall bounty hunter in his tracks. It sounded close but the long canyon had a way of playing tricks with a man's senses. The echoes seemingly went on for ever.

A deafening white-hot stream of lead lightning was fired along the canyon. Sunset narrowed his eyes and prayed that it did not seek his horse.

Sunset raised his left arm and pulled his hammer back as quietly as he could. He had travelled at least twenty yards since reaching the rockface but was that enough? The question haunted Sunset.

What if he was still out of range?

The tall lean man looked down at his shirt and pants. He was covered in blood and all of it was his own. He appeared to be draped in crimson. He swallowed hard and stepped away from the wall. He turned to the direction where he knew Carver had been standing.

For what felt like an eternity he saw nothing. A blanket of dense mist hung between them.

Then he heard the rifle being cocked again.

Although he could not see anything of the man he sought, Sunset fanned his gun hammer six times into where he had heard the Winchester being readied. Another rifle shot came back and ricocheted off a boulder to Sunset's right.

The bounty hunter shook the hot casings from his gun and started to walk to where he had seen the rifle shot come hurtling from out of the heat haze.

Within seconds he had pushed six fresh shells into his Colt, snapped it shut and cocked its hammer again. He paused and waited but the rifle did not fire again.

Sunset took a deep breath. Moss Carver might be dead, he thought, but then again he might be just waiting for the mist to clear so that he could take one final shot.

Sunset paused and listened for any hint of where the outlaw might be. Then he heard movement. The sound of boots on sand and then the snorting of a horse alerted the bounty hunter.

With no thought for his own safety Sunset ran forward through the fog. He saw the wounded Carver as the outlaw was about to mount his horse. The outlaw's left arm was bleeding badly and Sunset could see the bullet hole in the man's sleeve.

'Carver!' he yelled.

Carver swung round. Sunset saw the barrel of the rifle and fanned his own gun's hammer twice before it was levelled at him. The outlaw rocked on his heels, then slumped into the sands clutching his chest. Blood trickled from the corner of his mouth as the rifle fell to the ground.

The outlaw gave the bounty hunter a strange look.

'You do ride a black horse!' Carver said. 'I told Hope you rode a black horse!'

The lean man edged closer. 'Who do you figure I am, Carver?'

Moss Carver's head jolted back as he muttered his last word. 'Death!'

Johnny Sunset watched as the man fell face forward into the sand at his feet. He said nothing.

Finale

Nearly four hours later, when sitting astride his stallion, Johnny Sunset led the string of outlaw horses out from the mouth of the notorious canyon and into the rolling dunes on his journey back to Silver City. He had tied the bodies and the waterbags on to the animals, alongside the bags of paper money.

As the powerful horse meandered out into the fading sunlight the bounty hunter should have felt relieved that his work was at long last done, but Sunset knew there was a reason for the hairs on the nape of his neck to be tingling. His eyes searched the dunes all around him as the sun set closer to the horizon. Soon the red sky would be replaced by countless stars and then it would be impossible to see anything clearly. He shifted his weight and looked to either side of him as his mount walked slowly on.

Then he saw them.

They looked as though they had been waiting for some time as he approached. Even the fading light could not hide the gun grips both men had exposed in readiness.

Skeet and Will Bower had thought better of riding into the jaws of Deadman's Draw and decided that they would lie in wait to kill the bounty hunter should he be fortunate enough to survive the cursed canyon.

They circled the horseman and his caravan of packhorses like vultures waiting for death to give them a free feast. Neither rider seemed eager to get too close for a few minutes. It was only when Johnny Sunset reined in and stopped his mount to face them that the brothers decided to head towards the injured rider, who looked as though he had done battle with a mountain cat.

The Bower brothers hauled rein ten feet in front of the stallion's nose and stared hard at the horseman and his cargo of dead bodies.

'What you got there?' Skeet asked.

'What's it look like?' Sunset questioned.

Will Bower tilted his head. 'Looks like a whole lot of dead 'uns to me!'

'That's what it is OK!' his brother agreed.

The bounty hunter glanced at the sun. It was sinking fast below the distant sand dunes. The desert appeared to be bathed in red paint.

'What you boys want?'

'We're looking for the lowlife bastard who killed our brothers back at San Carlos!' Skeet snarled.

'They call him the Sunset Kid!' Will added.

Sunset smiled.

'You found him! What can I do for you?'

'We're gonna kill you for killing our kinfolk!' Will Bower grunted. 'Kill you dead!'

The elder Bower raised his hands until they hovered over his holstered guns. 'That's right! We're gonna kill you!'

Sunset nodded. 'You're wanted like your brothers! Dead or alive! Right?'

'Damn right!' both brothers said at the same time as their hands went for their guns.

The bounty hunter drew the scatter-gun out of the holster on his right hip and squeezed both triggers at once. He watched as the powerful weapon tore both Bower boys to ribbons and sent their bodies over the cantles of their saddles.

He reached back into his saddle-bags and pulled out two shotgun cartridges to replace the ones he had just discharged. He tapped the side of his horse and moved above what was left of the outlaws. It was a mess.

Sunset dropped the reloaded gun back into its holster and shrugged before patting his horse's neck. 'The gun works fine but I reckon I was a tad close there, boy! Ain't enough left of them critters to claim no bounty on! Figure the buzzards will have themselves a good feed come sunup though!'

The bounty hunter tapped his spurs and headed for Silver City leading the four heavily laden horses, behind him. The words of Moss Carver filled his mind as a myriad stars filled the sky above him.

'Death rides a black horse!' he repeated before adding, 'A mighty fine black horse!'

THE END

We do hope that you have enjoyed reading this large print book.

Did you know that all of our titles are available for purchase?

We publish a wide range of high quality large print books including:
Romances, Mysteries, Classics
General Fiction
Non Fiction and Westerns

Special interest titles available in large print are:
The Little Oxford Dictionary
Music Book, Song Book
Hymn Book, Service Book

Also available from us courtesy of Oxford University Press:
Young Readers' Dictionary
(large print edition)
Young Readers' Thesaurus
(large print edition)

For further information or a free brochure, please contact us at:
Ulverscroft Large Print Books Ltd.,
The Green, Bradgate Road, Anstey,
Leicester, LE7 7FU, England.
Tel: (00 44) **0116 236 4325**
Fax: (00 44) **0116 234 0205**

FAITH AND A FAST GUN

Chap O'Keefe

Joshua Dillard, the ex-Pinkerton detective, on a sentimental journey to a mission graveyard in Texas, had ridden into trouble. Guns blazed around the headstones as he intervened to save a girl called Faith from the clutches of Lyte Grumman and his gunhawks. Grumman, a cattle baron, believed that a rigged poker game had lost him a thousand head of longhorns. Now he was intent on recouping his loss, whatever it took — and Joshua's Colt Peacemaker was hopelessly outnumbered . . .

GUNS OF PONDEROSA

Chuck Tyrell

When Nate Cahill and his gang take over the town of Ponderosa, sawmill magnate Fletcher Comstock sends for his friend Matt Stryker. However, Cahill is waiting for him. He gelds Stryker's fine Arabian stallion and beats him terribly. But Stryker will not give up. He pins on the marshal's badge, tames a rowdy town and gets rid of the ruthless Cahill gang. Now the guns of Ponderosa blaze and blood runs red in the Arizona high country.

DEATH RANGE

Elliot Long

Bullet-scarred Jack Cain, through with cleaning up gun-crazy ranges and wild cow towns, heads for Montana to buy a small spread and raise cows. But a hundred miles up country, he encounters nine-year-old Ethan Wilder whose ma is shot and near to dying. Will he come and take a look? Reluctantly he agrees, only to find himself ambushed in a hail of bullets — but what follows next turns out to be Jack Cain's greatest test — but can he survive it?